GUNSMOKE AT ADOBE WALLS

Following the Battle of Gettysburg, army deserter John Terril escaped the firing squad by fleeing south. In Texas he becomes the victim of a crime, but after seeking vengeance he faces the hang-rope. However, Terril's escape from the penitentiary enables him to continue his pursuit of the murderous Diego Armijo. Avoiding arrest by the Texas Rangers, he trails his enemy to the Staked Plains — Comanche Indian country. At last Terril faces a showdown with Armijo — and gets his only chance of retribution . . .

MARK BANNERMAN

◆

GUNSMOKE
AT
ADOBE WALLS

Complete and Unabridged

LINFORD
Leicester

First published in Great Britain in 2006 by
Robert Hale Limited
London

First Linford Edition
published 2007
by arrangement with
Robert Hale Limited
London

British Library CIP Data

Bannerman, Mark
  Gunsmoke at Adobe Walls.—Large print ed.—
Linford western library
  1. Western stories
  2. Large type books
  I. Title
  823.9'14 [F]

ISBN 978–1–84617–736–1

Published by
F. A. Thorpe (Publishing)
Anstey, Leicestershire

Set by Words & Graphics Ltd.
Anstey, Leicestershire
Printed and bound in Great Britain by
T. J. International Ltd., Padstow, Cornwall

This book is printed on acid-free paper

*This book is dedicated
to my good friend
Bill Marriott*

Prologue

November 1867

Carpetbaggers: Adventurers from the North who rode into Texas after the Civil War in search of financial or political gain. The name is derived from the popular form of cheap luggage most of them carried — the carpetbag.

Terril was no stranger to blood. He had seen it spilled on the battlefield of Gettysburg. And now he felt it pounding inside his head, hastened by the race of his heart. Mixed with it was the echo of the shot that had caused his Galiceno horse Belle to rear and send him flying from the saddle. Thrown rearward, he had landed on his back, his fall broken by creosote brush. Though stunned, he was acutely aware

1

that a bullet had whined close to his head.

Now his ears registered laughter.

Two men, youngsters, stood grinning at him. One of them was brandishing a smoking shotgun.

Terril's attention swung briefly to Belle. The black horse stood ten yards down the trail, quivering and blowing, the whites of her eyes radiating fear. The carpetbag was still fastened across her withers.

Terril's nostrils widened to the taint of whiskey. Drink made his attackers even more dangerous.

They had stepped from the high, trailside brush. Both wore long black coats; they reminded Terril of vultures. One was tall, thin, knock-kneed. The other was shorter, with bulging girth; he waved his shotgun towards Belle.

'Bet you got a lot o' good things in that carpetbag,' he drawled. 'Far too heavy for that beast to carry, eh?'

His companion sniggered. 'Figure

we'll take a look, see for ourselves, try to ease the burden.'

Terril started to speak, but his tongue detected a fissure in his lip, caused by his own teeth in his fall, and he was again aware of blood.

'Don't,' was all he managed.

The man with the gun stepped towards the nervous horse, his watchfulness leaving Terril.

He had taken just three steps when Terril snatched his own gun from the pocket of his leather *chaqueta*. It was the percussion revolver that he had lifted from the corpse of a Confederate officer four years earlier. Now its blast brought a wild neigh from Belle, its charge spinning the ruffian around, a stream of blasphemies spilling from his lips. He had dropped the shotgun and now clutched his arm, his face contorted, blood a torrent through his fingers. He crouched, sickened, eyes radiating panic.

His companion also showed fear. 'We was only foolin',' he stammered out.

'We meant no harm. You could've *k-killed* Chet!'

Terril hauled himself up, wincing at his own pain, but none the less ensuring that the muzzle of the revolver remained in an arc between his adversaries. 'Get out, both of you!'

The two exchanged nervous glances followed by mutual nods, then they turned and stumbled away through the high brush. He was thankful that they had overlooked the fact that his revolver was no longer charged.

Terril recharged his weapon, giving the cylinder a quick spin to ensure that the caps were in place, at the same time listening to the receding passage of his attackers fading into nothing. Next, he set about retrieving the spooked Galiceno, together with the heavy carpetbag she bore. The carpetbag held his few necessities plus the multitude of pills, potions, medicines and medical supplies — Army surplus, from which he intended to make his living.

Having ridden southward through

Indian territories, John Paxton Terril had met his first Texan riff-raff.

He was a lonely man, a stocky twenty-two-year-old of average height. He possessed clean-chiselled features, black curly hair and wished nobody any harm. His mother had died in childbirth, his father, a colonel, and his elder brother had been killed during the war. Following the cessation of the conflict, he had come South, intent on seeking his fortune and starting a new life, trying to cast off the shackles of his past and the horror of Gettysburg.

But his first encounter with local Texas folk had been intimidating. Even more intimidating, he felt, was the speed with which he had drawn and fired his own gun. He'd sworn that the war had expunged from him all desire to take life.

The wounded ruffian's companion had said: *You could've k-killed Chet!*

And he'd been right.

1

September 1871

It was four years later and Terril had prospered under the patronage of the wealthy Mexican family which he had befriended, the Baltrans. During his early days in Southern Texas, a land of desert, mountain and high, arid plateau, he had impressed the widowed patriarch, Don Antonio Baltran. Don Antonio had helped in the founding of his store beyond the town of Ocatillo, close to the hot springs where visitors came to soak themselves in comforting waters; the young seeking recreation, others seeking relief from rheumatism, catarrh, urinary affections and female diseases.

He worked with a patience that was part of his strength, offering his medicines and supplies, frequently on credit. He catered for both physical and spiritual needs, everything from tooth-brushes to bismuth, spectacles to crucifixes and ergot to images of the Virgin Mary. He even stocked opium, which he sold to the old who were suffering from incurable illnesses. His prices were competitive and he imported only from reputable sources. Pedlars of medicines often departed quickly, fearing retribution for selling useless remedies, but with Terril it was different; his cures and advice worked and his clients returned for more. The medical skills that he had picked up while assisting surgeons during the days of Civil War stood him in good stead.

Today he was to be married. It was intended to be the happiest day of his life.

At the Church of Santa Maria, standing before rotund Father O'Kelly, he smiled at his eighteen-year-old bride and blinked to confirm he was not dreaming. Josefina Anna Claudine, the cherished daughter of Antonio Baltran:

she represented to him everything that was beautiful in femininity. Her dress was a startling white, with short puffed sleeves edged in lace. Her olive-complexioned face consisted of gently rounded lines, her mouth often showing the quick upturn of a smile. And today she had never looked lovelier because exultation danced in her green eyes. Acknowledging his glance, she murmured a conspiratorial whisper. '*Te amo*. I love you.'

For a moment, his mind drifted back to the first time he had seen her. One hot afternoon he had been returning from Galveston, driving his springboard laden with new purchases of medical stock. He had paused, setting his horse to forage, close to a secluded section of the hot springs.

Leaning back against a projecting tree-root, enjoying the shade and a cigar, he had been disturbed by feminine laughter. Believing themselves unobserved, a number of Mexicans had paused to enjoy a bathe. Servants were helping their mistress, a young woman, to disrobe. For the briefest moment, her gown had fallen open and he was afforded a glimpse of body, nubile breast and the wisp of pubis before her dignity was restored.

The blood pounded in his temples. For a moment, he could not breathe.

He carried the image of the girl into his dreams that night. He later learned her name was Josefina, daughter of his patron Antonio Baltran — and already premonition told him that he had encountered his future wife.

Now they were victorious, triumphant. He had courted her with all the chaperoned patience that was fitting, delighting in her skills with the guitar and her gentle singing of many songs, including his favourite.

There's a Yellow Rose of Texas
That I'm going to see

He became aware of a rival suitor, aware of his fury. Though he never met the man, the resentment he breathed was unmistakable.

The couple had beaten the odds in creating their union — the odds of his being an American of questionable past, a lonely man, a gringo to some, a trader in medicines who had gained respect with his honesty and fair dealing; not all carpetbaggers coming South had been unscrupulous. And of her being the flower of the wealthiest Mexican family in Ocatillo. She who was already promised to another man, yet had scorned him and chosen John Terril, initially against her father's wishes but ultimately with his blessing.

And this day they made their vows and he slipped the ring on to her forger, and the congregation tittered with excitement. They left the church arm-in-arm, radiating happiness, stepping out into the Texas sun, beckoned by hope for their future. Years enriched with passion, laughter and *bambinos*. Man and wife till God or death would part them.

He helped her into the two-wheeled *carreta*, a surrey, hauled by the ribbon-bedecked Belle. Terril was thrilled by his wife's touch, the closeness of everything he desired, the sweetness of her fragile scent, the warmth of a love finally unshackled from the eye of a chaperon.

Now it was that she whispered something to him: she had known that he had watched her when she had bathed at the lake, known that he had seen her nakedness.

They laughed together.

Following them, the congregation were conveyed in family-owned Concord coaches and on horseback to the hacienda of the Baltrans. Servants had set up tables in the yard, spreading them with turkey and vegetables covered in mole sauce; *tamales* cooked in maize leaves, frijoles and eggs *rancheros*. A steer and two hogs were turning on spits, emitting a rich aroma. Boards had been spread upon the ground for dancing. Close by, the wedding-presents were displayed: fruit bowls, fancy jugs, cushion covers, napkin rings and so on.

As the afternoon's heat relented, tequila brought an increasing abandon to the festivities. Guitars and castanets joined in frenzied crescendo, enticing family, friends and even rotund Father O'Kelly into the fandango.

Only when evening had waned and constellations of stars lay across the boundless sky did John Terril and his bride deem it seemly to take their leave. Amid congratulations, embraces and tears, they said *adios*, and embarked upon the half-hour journey towards home.

Terril had refurbished his white-washed house to the extreme that he could afford, painting the shutters and window-frames, purchasing curtains, carpet, a gilded mirror and a mural of Don Quixote tilting at windmills. It would be a fitting place to welcome his wife.

They had already stolen kisses, but

had remained sober, intent on allowing nothing to deny them the ecstasy of their prospective union. It seemed they had waited for ever.

★ ★ ★

Diego Armijo had worked steadily on his lever-action Henry rifle. Sweat had turned his shirt sodden. In the shade afforded by a shallow cave entrance overlooking the Hot Springs Road (an old Spanish trail) from Ocatillo, he had spent the entire afternoon cleaning and oiling the weapon's mechanism, polishing till they glistened the dozen silver studs that decorated each side of the butt. He continued far longer than was necessary, hoping it would take his mind away from the events at Santa Maria Church in town. It did not. Jealousy scorched his soul, causing him to grind his teeth and make the cords swell out on his neck. He mouthed a constant stream of angry oaths.

Let the carpetbagger have the girl.

They would soon be little good to each other.

Normally he favoured the knife as a weapon, but from a concealed position bullets would be the best servants. As for any retribution that might follow, he was not concerned. He had disappeared before into the vastness of Texas. He would do it again. The Texas Rangers represented the only real law in the territory, but he had no doubt that he could elude them.

The Henry, they said, was a weapon you could load on Sunday and fire all week. He slid shells into the chamber. He raised the gun, squinting through the sights at the road beneath him, knowing that he must be ready when the couple chose their time to slink back to Terril's home. He grunted with satisfaction. He was sure there would be no mistake.

Armijo was a heavily built, handsome man, with thick moustaches. He was thirty. His upbringing had been humble, but through his own effort he had hauled himself from the gutter, grafting and scheming, turning his charm on the prosperous and employing tactics that were seldom legal. However he had not shown the more devious side of his character to the wealthy Don Antonio Baltran and his family, instead pretending that he was a man of substance. He had seen in them opportunity; the daughter of marriageable age was a dalliance he would use. At first, Josefina had shown him the sweetness of her nature, only slowly sensing his true intent. By that time her father had promised her hand in marriage. By that time the carpetbagger had arrived.

Now Armijo eased himself down over the rocks, moving like a cat-footed Apache. He reached a rocky fissure, merging into shadow. He was now so close to the road that he would be firing at point-blank range. His impatience, his lust to destroy his prey, grew as he waited, his only companion a horned lizard. The afternoon declined into swift evening, the sun touched the skyline, melting into a final blaze before conceding to the night.

It was almost midnight when he heard the purposeful clip of iron-shod hoofs and saw, silvered by moonlight, the two-wheeled *carreta* approaching. Even at a distance Armijo admired the proud movement of the Galiceno horse hauling it, the ripple of light on its hide.

Still concealed, he spat, then settled himself against cold rock, his strong hands silently manipulating the lever action of the Henry rifle.

*   *   *

The road was deserted that night. It was generally quiet, except when customers to Terril's store flocked for his wares. Despite bearing the name of Hot Springs Road, the main concourse to the hot springs was further east.

After the shots had blasted off the only sounds beyond the reverberation came from hoofs and wheels as the *carreta* careered on. In panic, Belle drew the small wagon some fifty yards down the road, before, in her wild gallop, overshooting a curve. A moment later she had blundered into thick, thorny chaparral, where the vehicle toppled over, the wheels, one broken, spinning before eventually becoming still. Trapped in the traces, Belle tried to rise, frightened and snorting, but fell back, crippled by a broken foreleg.

Both bodies had been thrown clear, that of Josefina after the initial shot had shattered her head, that of Terril when the *carreta* came to final rest.

Quitting the rocks, hefting the gun, Armijo was surprised at how Josefina looked. Lying on her left side, the ghastly wound to her head concealed, she reminded him of an angel fallen from heaven. Had it not been for the blood meandering though the dust, she might have been asleep. A sentimental man might have been moved to tears. Instead, Armijo's teeth glinted in the moonlight in a triumphant smile.

He gathered her up as if she'd been a butchered carcass, hoisted her over his shoulder, walked down the trail to the spot where the vehicle had blundered into the chaparral, her blood glistening on his clothes. He was happy. Events would be concealed from anybody passing along the road. He found the body of Terril close by, dark with gore, partly impaled on thorns. He rested the girl down beside him. He doubted that the pair would find much solace in heaven.

The horse was threshing. He slipped the muzzle of the Henry beneath its ear and blew its brains out.

His final task was to drag the dust across the blood on the trail. He worked with his boot. The longer it took for anybody to discover the killings, the further away he would be.

2

Noon, Next Day and After

Not all creatures are tricked by concealment. Scent of carrion carries many miles to the highest thermals. Turkey-buzzards had gathered, appearing as a dark cloud in the sky. They hovered, their outspread wings motionless, their keen eyes penetrating even the thickest chaparral.

The first person on the Hot Springs Road next day was a physician. Doctor Nathan Hudson had magnificent sideburns. He was grey-haired, poker thin, well into his sixties and considering retirement. Unaware of the marriage celebrations, he was on his way to Terril's store to purchase bandages.

It might have been considered over-coincidental, over fortuitous, that a medico should be first to come upon the scene, but the truth is that even a doctor of the highest qualification can do little for the deceased.

Leaving his horse on the trail, he stepped carefully through the thorns, following where the vehicle had careered along. As he advanced, a familiar, sickening smell invaded his nostrils — death.

He came upon the horse first, a fine Galiceno, whose brains still clung to the splintered edges of the hole in her skull. Amid them, flies competed for foot-room. The animal, whom some knew as Belle, sprawled, still in the traces of the toppled, two-seater trap.

Further back in the chaparral, side by side, the bodies of man and woman lay.

Despite the flies and blood, it was clear that both still wore their finery — yes, wedding-clothes. The front of the woman's dress had been slashed to her navel revealing her pale young nipples. A closer examination told him that the exposing of her body had not played a part in her murder. It had been a separate deed of unspeakable debauchery, inflicted after the bullet had killed her.

Doctor Nathan Edmund Hudson MD was a graduate of medical college, veteran of battlefield, disease, childbirth, amputation without opiate, dissection of corpses, sickness in both male and female. Now, he retreated, crouched down amid the thorns, and would have vomited had his stomach been less immune. As it was, acid rose to his mouth. Feeling a sudden need for air, he removed his hat, wiped his forehead with his thin, trembling arm. He had never, never witnessed such . . .

And then came the sound.

It meant little to him, just a low animal-like moan, improbable, unexpected, and at first discarded from his traumatized awareness. A scavenger, maybe or . . . The sound came again, more insistent.

Only now did he turn and stumble towards the male body.

Recognition dawned in him. He

waved away the flies. Yes, here was John Terril, the Northerner, the former carpetbagger who ran the very store towards which the doctor had been heading.

With sudden urgency, he knelt by the body, fumbled for the pulse and felt its throb.

Hudson peered into the man's face and thumbed back an eyelid. Then he examined the bullet wound in his chest. He grunted with surprise. John Terril was alive, but for how long?

The doctor had to make a difficult choice.

He decided that here, even as a doctor, there was little he could do, apart from watch the man die. His best action, surely, was to go to his horse and fetch the velvet-lined satchel of medical equipment attached to his saddle. He would then administer what treatment he could, dusting medicinal flour into the wounds, bandage, cover his patient with a blanket, after which he would ride for Ocatillo to summon able-bodied help and a wagon. He could do little to distract the flies, but he consoled himself with the belief that at least the buzzards would not touch live flesh. Just how long that flesh would remain 'live' was a matter of conjecture. He knew the tidings he carried would hit Ocatillo like a bombshell, arouse seething emotion in the hot-blooded populace. But as he whipped his horse hell-for-leather through the shimmering heat, his concern was for the man clinging to life by his fingernails. *Please God, he prayed. Please God may we get back in time!*

* * *

When he arrived the town was committed to its siesta, the streets deserted and simmering in the heat, seemingly resentful of intrusion. But he encountered the town's undertaker, polishing his hearse. A coffin was already loaded upon it, ready for any exigency. A hurried explanation had the shocked man harnessing his two black horses, devoid of their normal plumes, and urging the hearse out along the road. It took the doctor another ten minutes to rouse townsfolk and spread word of the atrocity. Having changed his horse at the livery, he was soon leading a cavalcade of angry townsmen back along the way he had come, overtaking the hearse.

Meanwhile, news carried to the Baltrans.

★　★　★

Men scrambled into the chaparral. By nothing less than a miracle, Terril was alive, though still unconscious and balancing at the very edge of eternity. His attacker had left him for dead, which surely he would have been but for a quirk of fate. His wounds were terrible.

With gentle hands he was rested in the coffin, not because he had succumbed, but because, in the hearse, its satin lining provided the greatest comfort. Whether or not its lid was screwed down on arrival in town would depend on his condition. As for poor Josefina: male hands respectfully wrapped her body in a blanket. Her father, Don Antonio Baltran, had now arrived and under his distraught, tearful eyes, she was placed beside the casket.

Terril was taken to the Baltran home in Ocatillo. There, the last rites were spoken for him by Father O'Kelly. But on the fourth day, still unconscious, he showed signs of rallying.

Doctor Hudson inserted a makeshift chest-tube and expanded the collapsed lung.

Working with a colleague, he conducted an intricate examination. The first bullet had ploughed into the chest. With a scalpel and saline solution, he cut through muscle and ribs and explored the abdomen, probing to discover the exact nature of the damage. There was injury to internal organs, ruptured spleen, and slight laceration of the liver. The copper-jacketed bullet had exited through the back, causing haemorrhaging. Secondary damage had been caused by bone splinters. Striving not to overlook anything, the doctor feared peritonitis, infection, but found none.

The second bullet had been less considerate; it had lodged in the thick muscle of the shoulder. Hudson worked for an entire afternoon, removing it.

And on the fifth day the patient recovered consciousness. Though the room was curtained, he could see a pale-bodied Christ hanging on the wall, and could study the ornate ceiling — cherubs and nymphs cavorting on clouds. Amongst them, he imagined he saw the face of Josefina, her lips upturned in a smile, her eyes so dark and liquid and filled with love. *Te amo!* Pain stabbed at him and he returned to oblivion.

Meanwhile, as the Baltran family remained in deep mourning, Don Antonio was in no doubt as to the identity of his daughter's murderer.

Gradually, Terril's periods of consciousness lengthened. He started to take sustenance, chicken gruel, fed to him with a spoon by Josefina's sixteen-year-old sister, Florencia. At the end of a month, Don Antonio conferred with Dr Hudson, and it was agreed that Terril should be conveyed to the new infirmary in San Antonio to continue his convalescence. Baltran money would ensure that he had the best treatment.

3

Terril Returns

The cigar was the finest, imported from Cuba. But Terril could not enjoy it. Nothing gave him pleasure, for he was too angry, too bitter. Hatred dominated all other emotion. It was like a serpent coiling and uncoiling inside him. He quelled a tremor, forced himself to inhale deeply and lean back. It was warm September, one year after his wedding-day. He was seated, with Don Antonio Baltran, on the shaded veranda of the Mexican's hacienda; in the distance he could see a man training a mare in a corral. The animal was a Galiceno. It reminded him of Belle. Everything he saw or touched, even smelled, awoke some recollection of the night his wife had died.

'It is good,' Don Antonio said,

pouring whiskey into Terril's glass, 'that you have regained your strength.'

Terril nodded. 'I am grateful for your financial support and the good treatment of the doctors. But even the best doctors cannot cure what is in my mind.'

'Do you still have physical pain?'

'Pain in the ribs on the left side,' Terril said, 'and sometimes I get shortness of breath, but the doctors say I have been fortunate. Like you, it is my heart that has been wounded. I dream of him, dream that I am killing him.'

For a moment Don Antonio seemed unable to speak. A tear glistened in his eye. His hand was shaking as he raised his glass to his lips. He had aged visibly since the murder of his daughter, even developing a slight stoop.

After a moment he said: 'I blame myself for what happened.'

'Why?'

'I was fooled by the man. I should never have befriended him. I should have seen him for what he was.'

Terril drew on his cigar, but its richness tasted sour to him. He asked: 'Where is he now?' and then he spoke the name and it felt like acid on his lips. 'Where's Armijo?'

'He has a price on his head; it gets higher by the day. He killed two soldiers in Cimarron over a game of monte. He has formed a gang. They have committed robberies, more murders. The Texas Rangers have been hunting him ever since he killed Josefina. They cannot find him. Sometimes, I am sure, he goes far beyond Texas, beyond their jurisdiction. He needs to be found, hunted down, punished.'

Terril forced himself to be calm. 'I want to kill Armijo,' he said without emotion.

Don Antonio looked at him. 'I believe I have some information as to where he is.'

'What information?' Terril's interest quickened.

'I have friends who keep their eyes open,' the Mexican said. 'Sometimes they learn more than the law. And sometimes a single person, with anger burning in his heart, can be more effective than the law.' He stood up. 'I have a present for you.' He walked from the veranda, back into the house. Within a minute he had returned. He carried a rifle which he placed on the table before Terril. The weapon was brand-new and inlaid with finely tooled silver. 'I want Armijo killed with this weapon,' he said. 'It has become the very purpose of my life. I am sure it is what Josefina would have wanted.' He paused, then said: '*Por amor de Dios!* Terril, you have more reason than anybody to be his executioner.'

Terril felt excited. He placed aside his cigar and stood up. He lifted the Winchester, liking its balance. 'You mentioned money,' he said. 'You have already paid me. You have saved my life, paid for my recovery. It is I who owe you. Part of me died when Josefina died. In my dreams I have already killed Armijo. Now I will make it real.' He clutched the Winchester against his chest. 'I will kill him with this gun.'

Don Antonio sighed with anticipation. 'It is the newest gun produced by the Winchester Repeating Arms Company,' he explained. 'It can fire two shots a second. It is the most accurate weapon in the world.'

Terril said: 'You mentioned you had some information about his whereabouts?'

'*Sí*.' The Mexican nodded.

★   ★   ★

Terril's journey led westward through desert clothed in mesquite and cholla brush, following natural breaks in the ground. At night he lay in his blanket and listened to coyotes howl and felt the loneliness of the land. It was October 1872 and the inferno of summer had relented to the more merciful climate of the fall. He travelled light, just as he had when he had first come to Texas, everything he needed in his carpetbag. But now the Winchester, the very symbol of his determination, nestled in the saddle scabbard beneath his knee and he was no longer astride his beloved Belle, but the sturdy, Roman-nosed, Fedora, given to him by Don Antonio. In his saddle-bag was something else the Mexican had provided — a letter to one Dimaso Gondora, a tradesman who lived in the town of Laredo.

He travelled wary of Comanche and Apache raiders. Here, the country was green and he passed many *ranchitos*. He crossed the Neuces River and arrived in Laredo one Sabbath noon, just as the church bells were calling the faithful to mass. The town was big, a blending of Mexican and Texan cultures, and an enquiry led him to a small adobe establishment on the edge of town. Above its door was a sign: *Tienda Barata*, meaning cheap store. Within five minutes, he was seated in a back room, sharing tequila with the owner whose dog nestled against its master's leg, its doleful eyes showing deep love for him.

His host, Dimaso Gondora, was a short, wizened man, his smile revealing gold teeth. Terril passed him the letter which he read, then said; 'I will be pleased to help Don Antonio. For many years he was good to me.'

'You know where Armijo is?' Terril enquired.

The tradesman took a sip of tequila. '*Sí*. He bought supplies from me. But I had not got all he wanted. He was angry, told me I was a poor tradesman. He is not a kind man. I had to make a special import from Piedrus Negus. A month ago, I delivered it to his *rancheria*.'

'*Rancheria*?' Terril queried.

The other man nodded. 'It is in the Jaramillo Valley, just below the border, where the Texas Rangers cannot go. I can tell you how to get there. The journey will take no more than a day. I owe Don Antonio a favour.'

'Are the Mexican authorities not

interested in Armijo?'

Gondora shrugged. 'I do not think the *rurales* are interested in anything apart from tequila and women. Half of them are criminals themselves, always willing to accept a bribe. They are a joke.'

Terril nodded.

That evening Gondora prepared a map indicating a trail beyond the Rio Grande. He told Terril to take care, for the country was swarming with bandits. Terril was not concerned; any robber would find little of value on him. His only real asset was the Winchester, the horse he rode, and a little money.

He stayed with the Mexican overnight and next morning, after breakfast, saddled Fedora and rode out, fording the ankle-deep Rio Grande which slithered snakelike between the two countries; he had no problem with the uninterested, lazy official who manned the crossing. He prayed that Armijo would be at home and not rampaging out with his gang, intent on crime.

In the early afternoon, he came across a settlement and stopped at the trailside where a sign read: PABLO'S CANTINA and a fingerboard pointed the way. The place was decrepit adobe; an outside wall had fallen down and had been repaired with poles and factory cloth. The half-dozen customers inside seemed unconcerned by the prospect that the whole establishment might collapse at any moment. A man, obviously Pablo, stood drying plates, his bulging middle pressed against the bar. Terril ordered tortilla sandwiches and a bottle of Red Dog. Presently, as Pablo served him at a flyspot encrusted table, he mentioned that he was seeking work. And was he on the right road for Armijo's *rancheria*?

Pablo nodded, the smile sliding from his lips. His glance took in the Winchester at Terril's side. 'Armijo hires men,' he said. 'What is the work you do, *señor*?'

Terril felt the blood quicken in his veins. 'I do the same sort of work as Armijo does.'

The man frowned. 'Then you are not welcome here.' He gazed around, keeping his voice low. 'If you finish your food and depart there will be no trouble.'

Terril was taken aback. 'I can't understand. Has Armijo committed some crime?'

The man shook his head. 'Not in Mexico.' He turned away, clearly not wishing to continue the conversation.

Terril finished eating, paid and went outside. He refilled his canteen from a cask. He returned the Winchester to its saddle scabbard, conscious that he was being watched from the cantina. He mounted up.

What he had heard made sense. Armijo preserved his safety in Mexico by confining his outrages to north of the border.

4

Gunfire

The *rancheria* was small. Terril approached it through grazing long-horns, the tension growing in him. One thing was sure: Armijo was not going to parade himself to be shot. He might not even be home right now. In any event, Terril would have to be watchful, biding his time. He reined-in on a small hill, cloaked in trees. He dismounted, tethered his sorrel. He hunkered down, the Winchester across his knees and, shading his eyes against the sun, he studied the house. It had a red-tiled roof and was built like a fortress, its windows heavily shuttered — but its main door was open. Surrounding it were a number of outbuildings and a well. A man in a wide sombrero was working in the yard, stripped to the waist, prising out an old tree stump with an iron bar. It was not Armijo.

Terril could feel the hairs tingling on the nape of his neck. His breath quickened. He wondered how close he was to the moment he had dreamed about for the last year. The moment when he would be viewing Armijo through the sights of his gun.

The man had murdered Josefina, had nigh killed him, by firing from a hidden place. He deserved no better treatment himself.

Presently another Mexican emerged from the house, collected a horse from the stable and rode away. It was six o'clock when Terril saw dust rising to the east. Presently a group of horsemen materialized, all wearing sombreros and flared chaparreras. Several big dogs accompanied them.

Terril's gaze settled on the heavily built *vaquero* who led the party. They reined in in front of the house, the other men showing him obvious deference.

The name lingered on Terril's lips ... Armijo. He lifted the Winchester into his shoulder, enjoying the moment, but then a caution came upon him. He lowered the gun. Could he be sure that this man was Armijo? He had never seen him before. He peered at him. He had dismounted and was directing the other men with great authority. Even so, Terril reminded himself that he must make certain that this was the man he had come to kill.

He rose to his feet, not caring that he was now in full view. He walked steadily down the slope, the gun in his hands. So preoccupied were the Mexicans with their work that he was within twenty yards before they became aware of him. Then all eyes became focused on him, and voices were quelled.

Terril halted, standing legs astride, the rifle held ready. 'Which is Armijo?' he cried out.

The big man responded angrily, his admission tantamount to a self-inflicted death sentence. '*I am Armijo!* You

41

have no right to be here. What do you want?'

'You killed my wife!' Terril yelled.

Armijo cursed. Then suddenly he grabbed the big *pistola* tucked in his belt. The long-barrelled weapon was only partly drawn when Terril fired the Winchester.

His first shot narrowly missed. The second took most of the Mexican's head off in a flurry of blood. A third shot increased panic amongst the other Mexicans as they scampered for cover.

Elation filled Terril, like satisfied lust. He delayed no longer, twisting around and scrambling up the slope towards the trees where his horse Fedora was tethered. Behind him, he was aware of pandemonium — men screaming, horses neighing wildly, dogs yapping. Reaching the edge of the trees, he pulled up and turned.

Several women had rushed from the house, their alarmed cries sounding shrilly. One man, more composed than his companions, was kneeling close to the fallen Armijo, a pistol in his hands. Terril ignored him, swinging back towards his horse. His indifference cost him dearly. The crack of the gun came simultaneously with a whipping pain across the side of his neck and, reaching up, he realized that blood was pumping from a wound. He ploughed on, ripped Fedora's reins free of restraining brush. Struggling to calm the animal, he got his foot into a stirrup and hauled himself into the saddle. Still gripping the Winchester, he rammed hard with his heels, setting the horse surging forward. He needed to put space between himself and the killing, before pursuit was instigated.

He rode at full hammering stride, using a quirt, praying that Fedora would not stumble, forcing him across open country where cattle scattered from their path. He rode until foam slathered from the animal's mouth. At last he drew up. He gazed back but saw no sign that anybody was giving chase.

His shirt was wet with blood. He felt faint-headed. His bandanna was already sodden, but he untied it. Tentatively, he fingered his wound, satisfied himself that the bullet had only nicked him. He'd been fortunate. He refastened the bandanna as a makeshift bandage, hoping that the blood would clot; then he heeled his way on again, knowing that a mile or so ahead was a stream where both he and Fedora could find respite.

*   *   *

Terril forded the Rio Grande early next day at an unmanned point, returning to American soil. Seventy-two hours later he reported back to Don Antonio that the deed was done, that their beloved Josefina had been avenged. Both men experienced satisfaction, but not as profoundly as might have been expected, for nothing could bring her back. Don Antonio mentioned that a substantial financial reward had been offered for the killing of Armijo, but Terril was not interested.

He returned the Winchester rifle to Don Antonio. 'I pray to God, I'll never need to use a weapon like that again,' he said.

And so the matter could be closed — or so they thought.

Terril's neck-wound was healing slowly, and he would always bear a scar. He returned to his house. Apart from gathering dust, it was exactly as he had left it — ready to welcome Josefina. He opened up the shutters and felt renewed grief. If he had imagined that killing Armijo would refresh his soul, he was wrong. But over the next days, he started his business again, welcoming customers like old friends.

And then one Sunday, when he returned from church, he found a newspaper lying in the road and picked it up. It was a copy of the *Galveston Gazette*. His attention couldn't miss the main headline and that followed.

BRUTAL ASSASSINATION
IN MEXICO.

Mexican rurales have reported the murder of Fernando Armijo, a cattle baron. An assassin, said to be of American appearance, shot him down in cold blood at his hacienda in view of his wife and children. The family have offered a substantial reward for the capture of the killer — dead or alive! The motive for the killing is unknown, although there may be some connection with his older brother Diego, who is wanted on charges of robbery and murder.

Shock swirled through Terril like raw liquor. He blinked hard, reading the printed lines again to ensure that his eyes were not tricking him. He swallowed hard; the world seemed coated in green; he felt sick.

Por amor de Dios!

A voice inside his head screamed out: *You have killed the wrong man!*

★ ★ ★

A week later a stranger with bushy eyebrows rode into Ocatillo and made enquiries at the cantina. After his questions were answered, he said his name was Stolbred and he was a detective from the Pinkerton Agency. He could also have revealed that he was in the pay of the Armijo widow, but he chose not to. He slaked his thirst, then rode out along the Hot Springs Road, heading for the establishment of John Terril.

There, he charged Terril with the murder of Fernando Armijo. Terril felt utterly jaded; his eyes had sunk into hollows of shadow. His conscience had tortured him, plunging like a knife, deep into his soul. He had killed a man in view of his wife and children . . . was he no better than Diego Armijo?

Hearing Stolbred's accusation, desperation flared in him like terror in a wild animal. He turned his back on the detective, took a pace towards his percussion revolver resting on a nearby shelf. It was charged and ready. But he did not reach for it. Instead, he faced Stolbred again and held out his wrists. For the first time in his life, the will to fight had left him. The Pinkerton man snapped cuffs into place, checked they were secure. He nodded to Terril, gazing at him from beneath his bushy eyebrows with a look of pity. Stolbred was a kind man, but he was paid to do a job.

'We'll just get things sorted out here,' he said, 'the place made safe, the windows shuttered, your livestock sorted. It'll probably be a long time before you come back.'

'If ever,' Terril said grimly.

They had a wearisome journey ahead — and maybe a wearisome rope at the end of it.

5

Hanging Judge

Texas, at that time, had no extradition agreement with Mexico. It was therefore practice to bring to trial in San Antonio felons who had committed offences beyond its borders. The courthouse, presided over by Judge Jason Emerson, was gathering a reputation as a centre for harsh justice and multiple hangings.

For weeks, Terril languished in San Antonio's musty jail, an old military prison of hewed logs, where the ceiling was a scant eight feet high. It had been likened to 'the black hole of Calcutta'. It appeared overrun with industrious spiders. Through the barred window he could see the scaffold.

Meanwhile evidence was gathered and the legal chain set in motion. The trial was scheduled for early December, and witnesses, including the widow, would come from Mexico. Don Antonio, although not visiting Terril in jail, had a sound defence attorney appointed, and this man, Warren Reid, a grey-haired lawyer of considerable experience, sat in Terril's cell taking copious notes. He had a reputation for organizing logical defences and had saved at least three men from the gallows. However, he was a man of heavy sighs and didn't radiate much optimism.

Terril knew that, through lack of care, he had killed the wrong man. That the dead man had been a brutal and unscrupulous cattle baron, a bully, with a penchant for shady deals and trampling on others, was of little consequence. The Armijo family wanted justice and, in their eyes, the only appropriate justice was the hang-rope. Meanwhile the evil man who really should have gone to his grave was hidden in some remote hideaway, no doubt laughing as news of events filtered through to him.

During those grim days Terril had little appetite for food and he became thin, a shadow of his old self.

He had always been a lonely man. Losing his father and brother in the war had increased his loneliness. Looking back, it seemed that finding true love with Josefina had, for the briefest time, been like a candle burning in a fog of bleakness.

The wound in his neck had taken its time in healing. The local doctor attended him, but seemed little concerned with his patient. What was the point in fixing a neck when it was due for a stretching in the immediate future?

He had no visitors, although a church lady left him a jelly and a bunch of flowers. In early December he received a letter. It was from Josefina's sister, now seventeen.

Dear Señor Terril
We are sad for what has happened to you and watch for

51

*news. Papa is particularly con-
cerned. He spends much time
alone in his study. He blames
himself for not only befriending
Diego Armijo in the first place, but
also for setting you on the wrong
trail in search for justice. He has
done all that money can achieve
for your defence — but the Armijo
family are formidable. None the
less, we all pray for you and believe
that God, in all his wisdom, will
protect you through these grim
days. You, too, must pray.*

*Saludos
Florencia*

Terril had been at an all-time low.
The accidental killing had been a
terrible blow to him, had sucked the
will to fight from him. Fernando Armijo
might have been an unscrupulous,
brutal man, no doubt similar in nature
to his brother, but he had not been
breaking the law — and, as such, had

not deserved to be murdered. Especially not in view of his wife and children. Terril had been careless. He should have made certain he'd had the right man before firing the shots. There had been nothing to indicate that the man was not Diego — but he should have made extra certain.

And behind it all, he knew that his real enemy survived. The law seemed unable to run him down — and if he, Terril, went to the rope, Diego Armijo would continue to evade the justice he deserved, no doubt committing more outrage, inflicting more suffering.

Something of the old anger rose inside him. How different things could have been had his sweet Josefina lived! Why had God allowed such a thing to happen!

He allowed the fury to flow through him, seeking a calm beyond it. The truth was, he had been his own master. He had no one to blame but himself.

He read Florencia's letter over and

over. She might be a child, but her message provided a pinprick of light in his gloom. *You, too, must pray*, she had said.

Tomorrow he was to stand trial. He wondered if hell, should it exist, could be any worse than the predicament in which he now found himself. Before retiring to his cell-cot that night, he knelt and pleaded to God for forgiveness and strength.

* * *

The next three days would always be a blur in his memory. Proceedings took place in the old commissary building, reserved for trials. It still possessed loopholes for muskets used to ward off Indians. Terril felt like a galleon, adrift at sea in a fog out of which accusing voices blasted at him like fog-horns. The hateful face of Senora Armijo loomed before him, her words stabbing at him viciously. She was a haughty woman. Other Mexicans, witnesses to the killing, took the stand, their statements equally damning.

Two days were spent with the attorneys examining the witnesses.

Terril's defence lawyer, Warren Reid, argued with spirit, pointing out that Francesco Armijo had drawn his own gun at the time of the killing, that he would no doubt have shot Terril had the opportunity been there, also that Terril was driven by the most extenuating circumstances. But the odds were stacked against the defence. The prosecution, spurred on by the widow, young but strident in a way unusual for Mexican women, were hungry for a conviction. Conviction . . . with the rope beyond it.

And hovering above everything was the grim countenance of Judge Jason Emerson. He who had already sent eighteen men to death.

On the third day Terril was called to the stand. He knew that he was fighting a losing battle, that his plea of extenuating circumstances sounded thin.

Constantly pointing an accusing finger at him, the prosecutor hammered questions at him like bullets, giving him little opportunity for self-justification.

When Terril stood down, the attorneys went on to their summing-up, but offered nothing fresh in the way of evidence.

Finally Judge Emerson presented his summation.

'I think,' he said in a voice as heavy as doom, 'that when John Paxton Terrill was born into this world he already had the mark of Cain on him. He must have grown up like an untended bramble, his vices at first lying dormant.

'Our duty is to run down and ferret out the criminal classes and those who take the law into their own hands, to punish them in such a way as to be a warning to others who thus may be induced to direct their footsteps in another direction.' He then turned to the jury and said: 'I ask you to remember that this man is an assassin and has left a family husbandless and fatherless. The jury must now retire to consider its verdict.'

The members of the jury, local townsfolk, exchanged glances, then stood up and proceeded from the courtroom in solemn silence. It was an hour before they returned to take their seats. None of them met Terril's eye.

Their foreman faced the judge and said: 'We have reached our verdict, your Honour.'

'Guilty or not guilty?' the judge demanded.

'Guilty, your Honour ... guilty as sin.'

Some agitation ran through the courtroom, but Judge Emerson silenced it with his gavel. He now asked Terril to stand up, which he did. Terril knew what was coming, so he closed his ears and lost himself in thoughts of Josefina's smiling face, the sweetness of which was spoiled only by the self-important, pompous expression of the judge.

When he was led back to the jail he

had been sentenced to hang. There was, under Texas law, no right of appeal. The period of time between sentence and execution was usually one week.

★ ★ ★

He felt numbed, for the moment all emotion drained from his soul. He felt that his death would be an awful waste. He recalled the aspirations his father had held for both him and his brother, but all had ended in such tragedy. The terrible violence of the war had cost him dearly, had changed him from a youngster of mild disposition into somebody who had become familiar with weaponry and was prepared to take life.

Shortly after he was returned to his cell, a blacksmith arrived and a guard stood by. He was made to sit on the floor while leg shackles were fitted; their chain compelled him to take the shortest steps. The blacksmith had a truculent manner. 'Shackles won't come off until after you're hanged,' he explained with a smirk.

The days slipped by like sand through an egg-timer. Life now was immensely precious, every hour, every second, no matter how grim his condition. He realized it was something to which he'd never attached the value it deserved. He wished he could slow its passage. He needed time, time to compose himself, time to come to terms with all that had happened. But everything seemed to happen in a rush, night followed day, night followed day, and all he was left with was the consolation that soon he would be with Josefina.

He penned a letter to Don Antonio Baltran, declaring his sorrow for all that had occurred. He also wrote a note to Josefina's young sister, Florencia, thanking her for praying for him. The Lord moved in mysterious ways, he said, perhaps he would be kind to him on the other side. *Unless the Devil claims me first!* he thought. But he didn't express *that* possibility in the note.

He was visited by the padre, who spoke soothing words about how wonderful it was on the other side. If it's so wonderful, Terril thought, then why don't we change places, you go instead of me. However when he put the thought into words the padre merely shook his head. He left him a Bible with which to pass away his time. Terril did not want 'to pass away his time'. He felt a desperate urge to extend every second to its fullest extreme.

Then, on the afternoon of the fifth day, the local marshal visited his cell. He was a man whose belly overhung his belt. With a face as grim as a poker, he said: 'Prepare yourself for some news, Terril.'

Terril raised his weary eyes, his neck injury throbbing.

The marshal cleared his throat, then in a flat voice he announced: 'I guess your friend Don Antonio Baltran has some influential friends, and plenty of money to throw away. Your death sentence has been commuted to life imprisonment.'

Terril's head was in a spin. He wondered if he was dreaming.

'But when you get to that hell-hole Lexingford Prison,' the marshal went on, 'you'll wish you'd gone to the rope!'

Prison space in the San Antonio jail was needed. There was no delay. The following day Terril undertook the 200 mile journey to Lexingford prison under an escort of three armed marshals. He was still shackled, and in the company of two other prisoners.

Soon after arrival at the grim place he would be confronted with a stark reminder of his past — the looming figure of a man he'd hoped to leave behind for ever. A man of evil intent, who had started Terril's footsteps towards the nightmare of the hangrope and beyond. A man who would relish the prospect of resurrecting that nightmare.

6

Civil War

The sight of Lexingford county penitentiary was awful, the prospect of spending the remainder of his life there was beyond contemplation. As the wagon conveying the new prisoners trundled in, the great iron gates closed behind them with a deafening clang. Heavily armed men patrolled the galleries, from which the constant cries of prisoners could be heard, a depressing sound that hardly stopped night or day.

Still shackled, Terril was forced with others to stand in line while details were recorded by a clerk with meticulous care. Then, each was given a number. After this, they were forced to shuffle along to a storeroom where prison suits were issued.

And it was there that the looming, black-bearded Sergeant Rainbolt stood, as foul-mouthed as ever, ordering his underlings about as if he was still at Gettysburg. He was a prisoner, but had obviously risen to some position of responsibility and now was making the most of it, his voice bellowing, sending other prisoners scuffling about with armfuls of prison suits. When he turned and his eyes met Terril's, his great jaw sagged and then, with realization dawning, a leer crept over his face.

'Private John Terril,' he said, 'at last they've caught up with you, so you can face up to what you deserve. And fate has put me here to make sure you get it. No running off like a scared rabbit this time!' The leer disappeared from his face. He gestured to the scar that formed a purple line across his temple. 'You did this, my friend. You nigh blew my head off . . . but not quite!'

Terril ignored him, taking the suit that was offered. He held it against himself. It was about three sizes too small, but he would not complain.

Rainbolt pointed a finger at him. 'I want this one to have the extra special treatment,' he called out. 'The very extra special treatment!'

The remark brought mocking laughter from his companions and a general nodding. 'His life won't be worth living,' somebody remarked.

A kick caught Terril in the back of the knees and he was pitched forward. He scrambled up amid hoots of mirth. Somebody, a prison guard, grabbed his arm and forced him along a gallery. Prisoners stared at them from behind the bars, their arms dangling through.

'Could be they'll forget to take them shackles off you,' his guard said. 'Sometimes Sergeant Rainbolt bribes us guards to forget.'

Five minutes later Terril found himself one of four in a small, dimly lit cell. The other inmates made no effort to greet or welcome him. The whole atmosphere smelt of excrement and urine — not surprising: an overflowing bucket supplied the only sanitation.

The sight of Rainbolt had been a shock to him. For years he had imagined that those grim days, when Rainbolt had endeavoured to make life an even worse nightmare, were gone.

Terril slumped down against the wall, the shackles paining his legs as they had done ever since his sentence was imposed. Would Rainbolt really 'arrange' that nobody gave a thought to their removal?

His mind touched upon Josefina, as it so often did, then roamed further back, recalling the nightmares that had forever remained in his mind, seeking the opportunity to flood back upon him. The most dreaded word he had ever known pounded in his head. To him, it was like a blasphemy — *Gettysburg*.

* * *

It was July 3, 1863. The third summer of conflict.

Terril flinched at the volley of shots; it seemed he was sharing the awful impact of lead against flesh, the oblivion of death that followed. This was no battle. Three men had stood bare-chested, blindfolded, their hands bound behind them. Then the ragged blast from the firing squad had come. Fleetingly, faces were contorted, then they were gone for ever, leaving an image of shock and bloodied flesh. An example had been set. They would never desert again.

It was an odd time to conduct executions, to kill your own men when the enemy was about to attack in overwhelming force, but Federal General George Meade would tolerate no more cowards and shirkers, no more mutineers, and so had set the example.

Today was the twentieth birthday of John Terril; it was also the day on which he learned about his father. Terril had been resting his back against a tent pole, weariness sapping his strength, when, amazingly, an orderly had found time to distribute mail. A letter had come from his uncle in Maine. He tore it open, scanned its message. It slipped from his hands as its news seeped into his brain. He slid down onto his haunches and wept. His brother had been killed at the very outset of the war . . . and now his father too, by a sniper's bullet at Chancellorsville.

He put his hand to his head, unknowingly smearing it with blood. Fifteen minutes earlier, 200 yards back at a field hospital, he had been administering opiates while an over-wrought surgeon amputated a man's arm. There was too much blood, everywhere was blood — and tattered flesh. Flies were drawn by effluvia, filth and body waste. Men had been crushed, maimed and cut by days of battle. Scarcely had the operation been completed when the order came through that medical orderlies were to report to the front line to help repel the coming onslaught from the Confeder-ates.

In the background he could hear Sergeant Rainbolt bawling orders, haranguing men. Sergeant Rainbolt of the huge black beard and overbearing presence. Suddenly the bully's attention was focused on Terril. 'Get up, you lazy hog. This ain't no rest camp! Just 'cos your father's a colonel don't hold no sway with me!'

'My father's dead,' Terril said.

If Rainbolt understood the implication of the words, he ignored it. 'Don't you have no lip for me. There's seventy-thousand Johnny Rebs out there, and all you can do is sit on your arse!'

Rainbolt turned away, shouting at somebody else, moving off between the tents.

Yesterday, the second day of the battle, the Federal Army had retreated and deployed onto the high ground west of the town called Gettysburg, and was now preparing for another onslaught from Robert E. Lee's Rebel hordes. It was said this battle could end the war. Scouts had reported back that the enemy were 'thick as fleas'. True enough. Terril, standing on Cemetery Ridge, had peered through binoculars, down across rolling meadows and groves of trees baked by the hot sun. It seemed that the entire Confederacy, mounted and on foot, was advancing like a grasping hand towards the ridge, the dust clouding up, pipes shrilling, drums beating, its flag, blue cross on red, swirling like a taunt.

Later, the advance was to become known as 'Pickett's Charge'. Today it was simply hell on earth. Victory for the Rebels would leave a clear road to Washington.

Terril rested his smooth-bore musket on the stone wall before him; he was part of the defensive line just forward of the summit of Little Round Top; every man had been issued with sixty rounds of ammunition. Some of them had stacked up small mounds of cartridges in front of them. He wondered how many of those alongside him would survive this day ... whether he, himself, would join his father. The air was incredibly humid. The sun burned them, for there was no shade, but the cover of the wall was more important than shade. From behind, cannon had opened up, sending salvoes over their heads to burst amongst the enemy. Enemy fell, but this seemed only an inconvenience. They came on, like hot treacle flowing relentlessly, filling every gap as it appeared in their ranks. There were 70,000, Rainbolt had said. The whole of bloody Virginia!

The artillery barrage was growing in intensity, shot cleaving the air over Terril's head, coming from both Federal batteries and those supporting the enemy advance. The racket was so deafening that some men covered their ears. Shells landed just behind the defensive barricades, spuming earth skywards, shaking the ground, having shrapnel whizzing through the air, the smell of cordite like gas. Smoke hazed the battlefield, clinging about the advancing figures, making them appear as black demons emerging through the swirling white. Even so, Terril could see that many had fixed their bayonets and that officers were brandishing swords aloft.

The Confederates had reached a long fence that crossed the field; horsemen leaped it, foot soldiers clambered over, undeterred by pounding artillery. Much of the fence had come down. The man next to Terril said: 'That won't please the farmers none. Both sides agreed they wouldn't damage fences beyond the top rail!'

'Could never understand that,' somebody else remarked. 'Take the top rail away, and the next one becomes top!'

Now the Confederate pace increased; they moved at double-clip across a cornfield, and as they progressed into rifle range the artillery subsided. Men had dropped out there, lying amid sheaves of wheat, riderless horses milling, but still the survivors came on.

Now the order was passed down the

centre line: 'Ready!' and muskets were pulled into shoulders. 'Aim . . . Fire!' Willing fingers tightened on triggers, sending forth a blast of lead. As ramrods flashed, men of the second rank made ready, firing a further volley.

Terril worked tirelessly, his hands tremulous and sticky with sweat. He brought each cartridge up, ripping the paper with his teeth, pouring powder into the upturned muzzle, forcing home the charge with his ramrod. Fire, recharge! Fire, recharge! Working feverishly, he took aim as best he could, but could not be sure whether he was hitting his target. And all the while the enemy were getting closer, closer, emerging as individuals, their faces twisted with hatred.

Before the wall the ground was thickening with bodies of men and horses. Those on each side of Terrill were slumped down, their blood drawing flies. Another man was crying out with pain as he clutched his leg.

And then the wall was breached and

the Rebels came surging through across rocky ground, using bayonets and rifle butts to murderous effect. Terril clouted away a Confederate corporal with a swing of his musket, then shot another man who lunged at him. Ferocious hand-to-hand combat ensued, muskets swung by their barrels, faces thrust into each other. Men grappled and died and stumbled over each other in confusion, the only differentiating factor: the blue of Federal uniforms. As for the Rebels, some wore grey, but most were in their farm clothes — and at any rate, it shortly did not matter, for everyone was tattered and bloody as they trampled on fallen bodies.

The Confederates swarmed on, advancing beyond the wall, screaming their Rebel cries. But suddenly Federal re-enforcements streamed down from the summit of the hill, and the advance faltered. Gradually, it was reversed. Rebel flags lay trodden on amid the bodies. As the tide turned, Confederate determination faltered until a rout set in. Men, many wounded, staggering in retreat, clambered over the wall and fled in disarray, not looking behind as they limped through their fallen comrades.

Gradually, quiet settled over the ridgelines, fields and woods. The carnage they called the Battle of Gettysburg was over.

* * *

That evening, in the stunned silence of afterbattle, Terril was ordered back to his medical duties. Clutching his satchel, he was stepping through the corpses that blanketed the field, when his attention was aroused by a cry. Moving across, he recognized the twin collar-stars of a Confederate officer. He stooped low; the man was a gory mess, clearly dying, but now his lips formed a plea for water and Terril uncorked his canteen, supported the man's head, and poured water into his mouth.

It was then that the vicious crack of a

pistol sounded. The officer's head erupted into a mass of gore and brains, torn from Terril's supporting hand. Terril spun round, his ears reverberating with echo, his face splattered with blood.

Sergeant Rainbolt stood a few yards away, his bearded face creased in a leer. 'Rebel shit!' he snarled. 'Don't need no water!'

Terril noticed the big percussion revolver that the officer was clutching in his lifeless fingers. On impulse, he grabbed it and pulled it free. Rainbolt took it as a threatening gesture and immediately pointed his own gun at Terril, the whites of his eyes glinting with madness. Earlier, Terril had seen him plundering corpses, going through pockets and taking anything of value.

Terril was sickened by the sergeant's behaviour but he intended no aggression. Rainbolt had been looking for an excuse to vent his anger but, frustrated with Terril, he turned. His glance took in two horses, Confederate horses, survivors of the battle, tethered close by. Without hesitation he fired his gun, shooting one animal through the head, dropping it immediately.

The leer had returned to his bearded face. 'Rebel shit!' he repeated. Then, seeking to reestablish his authority over Terril, he said: 'You got that fancy new gun! Shoot the other damn horse.'

Terril's gaze swung to the animal. It was a fine Galiceno mare, black as night. He gripped the butt of the pistol firmly.

'No,' he said.

'I'm ordering you to, Terril!'

'No!' Terril repeated, and seeing fury about to explode in the other man, he raised his pistol and fired, sending Rainbolt falling back.

Without further thought he jumped across to the Galiceno, ripped its reins clear of the restraining brush, rammed his foot into the stirrup and hauled himself into the saddle. He did not look back but he heeled away, leaving the battlefield behind. He rode hard, on and on, until the encroaching dusk settled down about him. He then stopped at a stream, watered the horse and washed himself, fearful at what he had done.

*　*　*

For the next week, he kept to the Pennsylvanian wilderness, living off the land, not even seeking sustenance at the farmhouses he passed. He knew that there would probably be patrols out seeking deserters, that, once caught, his only fate would be the firing squad. But gradually he progressed south, keeping to the back trails and staying on high ground where possible, avoiding contact with other humans. He still had his satchel of bandages and medical supplies, and once he came across a deserted field hospital. In cupboards he discovered further medical supplies and medicines. He also found another satchel; he gathered as much as he could carry, believing that it might provide him some benefit.

He kept a wary eye open for pursuit, but as summer waned into the fall, he was far to the south. His only companion, his only friend, was the horse. He had named her Belle.

Deep into the Indian Territories, he became bolder, even taking long-term employment at a farm. And time slid away, months turned into years, and news came through that the Confederacy had surrendered. Robert E. Lee had thrown in his hand at the Appomattox Courthouse. The war was over.

7

Disease

The first case of diphtheria was diagnosed at the penitentiary after six months of Terril's imprisonment. A young Mexican prisoner, confined on the third floor, developed a fever and throat infection that at first was not considered significant. But within a week the symptoms were spreading to other prisoners at an alarming rate and the upper floor of the prison was sealed off. John Terril had seen how others became institutionalized, but he still inwardly rebelled against the system, swearing to himself that sooner or later he would break free. Daily chain-gangs went out to the adjacent stone quarries and saw-mill, and although his muscles became strong, his physical health was not enhanced by the wretched diet and appalling conditions of hygiene which they were forced to accept.

He was not uncommunicative or reclusive, but even so he generally kept within himself, living with his memories and thoughts of what might have been but for the depravity of fate. He heard little from outside the prison, but bent to the strict discipline imposed, making the noises and responses that would bring him least trouble.

Fortunately, he was accommodated on a different level from Rainbolt. He saw the man frequently enough, even heard his bullying voice, but he managed to avoid him to a large extent. However, he was aware that the former army sergeant had not forgotten the incident at Gettysburg and still held a grudge. He would wave his fist at Terril in the exercise yard, and Terril knew he was just waiting for his chance. He learned that the sergeant had been confined following the murder and rape of a woman in Dallas. There must have been some extenuating circumstances, otherwise the sergeant would have gone to the rope, but of these Terril never became aware.

It had been six months before the authorities realized Terril's medical aptitudes and soon after this, he was consigned to the prison infirmary, where he spent his working day nursing the sick. He was thus aware of the alarming spread of diphtheria, seeing men coughing and spluttering, fighting to swallow and breathe, their airways obstructed by membrane growth. It was no surprise to him, for the filthy conditions were an invitation to infection; it was all too easy, in the crammed conditions, for the poison to be spread into the bloodstream. At first, the prison governor refused to admit that there was a problem, so there was a delay before the terrible contagion was recognized. But when the first fatalities occurred there could be no more denial. Some men died from the dreaded disease, others from the heart attacks it induced.

Effort should have been made to evacuate men to outside accommodation, but those who might have effected this measure failed to do so. It was impossible to provide isolation within the prison walls. Before long, the infirmary was overflowing, the beds of patients crammed side by side, so that containment of the disease was impossible. Some patients poked fingers into their mouths, trying to wipe away the growth in their throats.

Terril worked tirelessly, a rag pulled across his face, tending the dying, seeing his fellow orderlies struck down. He himself feared for his own fate, dreading the onset of throat soreness and fever, but that did not prevent him from doing his utmost to help others. He saw it as a way of atoning for the terrible sin he had committed, praying that the good Lord would observe his dedication and show mercy.

The penitentiary had now been closed to all further admissions. It was sealed off from the outside world, a place to be avoided. Each morning, bodies were removed by the cartload, being taken to a morgue for cataloguing before burial in the prison cemetery. As more prisoners succumbed, the grim corridors on the upper floors echoed with emptiness, while the ground floor was used as an expanded infirmary.

Then one morning, three weeks after the initial outbreak, Terril felt the first tingle of soreness in his own throat.

As a deceased patient was removed from his bed, another man took his place, a large man whose great beard had become tangled and messy with the phlegm he had brought up. The glands in his neck were swollen. His eyes were wild, frightened, and when they touched upon Terril the look of fear increased.

'I'm dyin',' Rainbolt said. The once booming voice was a raspy whisper, and speaking caused a terrible bout of coughing to erupt. He was left fighting for his breath, panic stamped across his face.

Rainbolt looked as if he was collapsing inward on himself. Terril turned away from him, knowing that there were other tasks to attend to, other patients to care for.

Throughout the day, Rainbolt lay writhing in distress, his face turning blue, his hands cupping his jaws, trying to draw air into his lungs. A harassed doctor, wearing a surgical mask, stooped over him in brief examination, but soon stood back, shaking his head. 'Nothing to be done', he said. 'Nobody can help him but the Lord.'

Terril overheard the words. For a moment his gaze rested on the man who had turned events at Gettysburg into an even greater nightmare for him. It grieved him to see any living soul in such distress.

'I think there is something we could do,' he said. 'I saw it done in army hospitals.'

'There's nothing,' the doctor said, annoyance flaring in his eyes that a mere orderly and a criminal should advise him on medical matters.

'I'll need a scalpel,' Terril said, ' . . . and a throat pipe.'

The doctor looked at him with bemused eyes. 'It won't work,' he said. 'Don't expect me to help you.' But he pointed. 'In the cupboard over there. You'll kill him.'

'You say he's dying anyway,' Terril nodded, 'so there's nothing to lose.' He turned to the cupboard.

The doctor watched him for a moment, then shrugged and turned to another patient.

A moment later Terril slapped Rainbolt across the face, the shock stopping his writhing, and causing his eyes to register incredulity. Lying motionless, he could have been dead and would be soon if Terril did not act quickly.

He climbed on top of the sergeant, his knees forced down on the man's shoulders. Using scissors he trimmed away a mass of filthy beard, baring the throat. With his fingers, he located the thyroid gland, then, taking a deep breath, he plunged the scalpel through the cartilage below the Adam's apple, striving to avoid injury to the neck. With blood flooding over his hands, he forced the pipe into the hole, into the windpipe, and then bound it around with bandage. Rainbolt's eyes were wide, his struggling returning; he tried to speak but merely gurgled.

Air surged into his lungs. He reached for Terril's arm, clawed on to it. Again, he tried to express words and failed, but his eyes spoke for him. They were deep pools of gratitude.

There was no guarantee as to how long he would survive, but at least he was able to breathe now.

Terril once more became aware of himself — the swollen, blistered feeling in his throat, the rising fever. He tottered a few steps, would have fallen, but steadied himself against a table.

Presently he stumbled into an ante-room where corpses were laid out. No other living soul was present. He was suffering double vision and burning with fever. He needed to rest. He found himself a sheet, wrapped it around his body, then he lowered himself on to the floor. He suspected he was dying, that soon he would find either perdition or salvation. He lost consciousness.

His senses returned. He was in a different place. He was lying on his back. His fever seemed to have abated. He could hear men's voices, not close but at some distance. He tried to swallow, succeeded. He determined to stand up and thrust his hands downward on to the floor. He realized that the corpses surrounding him were placed in orderly lines. He saw an open door at the end of the room. Sunlight was streaming through it, highlighting thick dust. He moved unsteadily forward, taking care with the placement of his feet. The voices continued. He reached the doorway and passed beyond into a street. He forced himself to walk quickly.

8

Armijo

'You should not ride so fast, Florencia,' the servant woman Maria said. 'One day you will fall off.'

Maria and her young mistress, Florencia Claudia Baltran, had dismounted by a small river, the Caballa, to rest their horses. They took a ride each morning across the family ranchlands which extended over rolling hills and prairie, shaded by sycamore and oak. Florencia, nineteen, was bright and frolicsome, eternally smiling. Her father, Don Antonio, had placed in her all his hopes for the future. Now she glanced at her reflection in a pool close to the stream. She wished she had been blessed with her late sister's beauty, but it was not so, although youth and exuberance ensured her attractiveness.

'I am not afraid, Maria,' she said. 'If I fall off I shall get up and get on again.'

She had assumed the role of eldest child in the family with grace, a credit to her father and to the memory of her mother, blossoming into womanhood with confidence. Riding side-saddle, she knew she was an excellent horsewoman. The smooth, rocking motion of her mount's steady lope carried stimulation into every part of her body. She suspected that Maria only complained because she could not keep up.

Her father, Don Antonio, guarded her with jealousy, fearful of her forming a liaison with an ill-suited man. He had never recovered from the loss of Josefina and frequently viewed the outside world with suspicion. She knew he felt desperately guilty about the part he had played in the killing of Fernando Armijo. Had John Terril spoken out at his trial, he could have easily been implicated in the crime. But Terril had never mentioned his name and was suffering punishment for both of them.

At least Don Antonio had used his influence and money to have the death sentence commuted, but there was nothing he could do to alleviate the prison sentence. Meanwhile, Florencia knew that stories were rife of Diego Armijo's exploits. Bank and stagecoach robbery, murder, even rape had been attributed to him and the gang he had formed, handbills had been spread across the state appealing for his arrest, the State Legislature had authorized substantial rewards for his capture and bounty hunters combed the land — but nobody could run him down.

Maria kept a pocket-watch which she now consulted. 'It is time we got back,' she said. 'Your tutor will arrive shortly.'

Florencia breathed in deeply, refreshed by the cooler, autumnal air. The sky was a cloudless blue. She loved this spot, at the edge of her father's domain, where the wandering river took a double curve. The current had eroded the bank, creating a cliff of red rock, and then, as if on a rebound, had done the same on the opposite side. She could see a deer watching them from the nearby oak trees. Suddenly the animal jerked nervously and darted off into the shadows.

Uneasiness touched Florencia. What had scared the animal? The horses, too, were showing nervousness.

She did not know that they had been observed — ever since they had left the hacienda.

Florencia screamed as a man in a large sombrero appeared from the riverside rocks, his pistol raised towards them. He was swarthy, dressed in a skin poncho, like an Indian, but he had a shaggy moustache and was clearly Mexican. She had never met Diego Armijo, but her mind had always been filled with stories of his evil deeds. Now, instinct warned her that she was at his mercy. She and Maria clung to each other in fear.

★　★　★

The fever raged in Terril, yet he forced himself through the wooded terrain south of the prison and morgue, soon reaching country that was sparsely populated. He did not fear pursuit at this stage. Conditions in the prison were far too dire for the authorities to concern themselves over individuals. One prisoner less would mean one less carrier of infection. But he had no doubt that records would exist and when a check was eventually made of those who had been identified and buried, against those prisoners who survived, his absence would be noted and information passed to the Texas Rangers. They had a reputation: to 'ride like the devil, track like a Comanche, shoot like a Kentuckian and fight like the devil'. But Terril knew that a greater risk was currently posed by the disease. He had no desire to infect others by seeking help from local folk, so he found himself a niche. He waded along a winding stream until he found a secluded stand of willows and there fashioned a rough shelter from branches. Within a bower of leaves, he rested for a week, feeling the fever rise towards a delirium in which the past paraded through his mind with all its grim horror — Gettysburg, Armijo, the prison and, then, one day, he was aware of Josefina smiling at him, whispering *Te amo*. She was fingering the strings of her guitar and in her gentle voice began to sing:

There's a yellow rose of Texas
That I'm going to see . . .

And he was suddenly laughing, as they had laughed that time ago.

He felt hysterical, in a dream world, filled with people with bulging eyes staring at him. At one point he rose through the mists of nightmare, to hear voices and gradually it came upon him that what he was experiencing was reality. The bushes about him moved, and several men, farmers, pulled up, gazing at him. They were big men, seeming as tall as the trees. Some of them had guns.

'Looks like he's escaped from the prison,' one of them said. 'Still got his fancy prison suit on!'

Anger stirred Terril. He reared up before them, shaking with disease.

'Don't come near me,' he shrieked out. 'I got plague.'

For a moment they appeared confused, then they backed off and shortly he heard their scrambling departure. They did not trouble him further.

When the fever broke, drenching him with sweat, he realized that he would not die from disease. His throat had lost its thickness, and he felt desperately hungry. Several hours later, to his astonishment, he managed to catch a sluggish fish from the river with his hands and, having no means of making fire, he was obliged to eat it raw. But it gave him some sustenance, and the following day he felt certain that he was beyond the infectious stage. He went to a farmhouse, where a lady, taking pity, gave him a good meal. He chopped kindling for her in exchange.

He did not linger but struck south, earning recompense for small tasks he undertook at farms. Whenever questions were asked, he moved on, his strength growing with each day.

He looked to the future. Assuming he could avoid recapture, he knew he must re-establish contact with Don Antonio; he had nobody else to turn to. Of course his presence would bring danger to the Mexican, so he would have to be careful.

Three weeks later, in the dead of night with the winter stars high in the sky, he approached the *rancheria* from the north, riding a weary nag for which he'd traded. The lights of the main house were out. He crossed the yard, memories of the gaiety of his wedding-day flitting through his mind. What changes time had brought . . . He went to the servants' quarters, roused a startled peon, and within ten minutes he was with Don Antonio, who embraced him affectionately, hardly able to believe his senses.

'You look gaunt and wild, *amigo*,' he said. 'You look as if you have been living like animal.'

Soon Terril was sitting in the main room, a tray full of food before him.

There was no jollity in the Mexican; he looked even more drawn and saddened than he had done at their last meeting. Of course Terril explained his horrific experiences and Don Antonio listened with great patience. And then he revealed the startling events that burdened his own mind. 'Three weeks ago, Florencia was out riding.' He placed a distraught hand to his forehead. 'But she never came back.'

'My God!' Terril shuddered. 'The servant girl, Maria . . . she came back alone, the following day. She was in a terrible state. She had been raped . . . by Armijo's men. They were a rough crowd. Some were half-breed Indians. She thought they would kill her, but she escaped.'

'And Florencia?' Terril interrupted.

Don Antonio shook his head in despair. 'He's got her. Armijo's got her. God knows what he'll do with her. I have my men out, scouring everywhere. The Texas Rangers have been hunting too. They reckon he has made a lot of money, trading guns to the Indians, maybe up north of the Red River. My God, that's really wild country, roamed by the Comanche. That is no place for my sweet Florencia.'

* * *

For a moment he was overcome with emotion. His head slumped; shudders took hold of his body. Terril reached out, rested a comforting hand on his shoulder. He could hardly believe the story he was hearing.

At last Don Antonio went on: 'I feared the man would come back one day. I knew he would never forgive me for having scorned him. Not even the murder of dear Josefina would satisfy his lust for revenge. I could not keep a constant guard on Florencia every minute of the day. She is such a high-spirited girl, with a determination to lead her own life. It was impossible to keep watch on her all the time.'

Terril shook his head in despair.

'Have you heard any word of her since she went?'

Don Antonio's face was a picture of misery. 'Nothing,' he said. 'Not a sign. I wondered if he might contact me, demand money. I would have paid to get her back. But I have heard nothing — and I have concluded that it is not money he wants, just revenge. She may already be dead. If that is the case, then I pray that somehow her body can be brought back, that at least I can bury her beside her sister and mother.'

Terril drummed his fingers on the table in anguish. He did not know what to say. The food lay unfinished before him. His hunger was forgotten.

'I went to Austin to the headquarters of the Texas Rangers,' the Mexican

98

went on. 'I spoke with the Headquarters Officer himself, pleaded with him. They have tried to help, but their powers are limited. They have other cases to follow up. There is only so much they can do. And they have big trouble with the Indians, with the Comanche. Their chief, Quanah Parker, is raging all-out war against the whites.'

'I must keep clear of the Rangers,' Terril said. 'If they find out about me, they will arrest me. I must avoid them at all costs.'

Don Antonio nodded.

Terril felt the hatred hardening inside him. 'I must go after Armijo. I will know no peace until he is dead.'

Don Antonio looked up. 'I will give you all the supplies you need, everything. This time there must be no mistake.'

'There's something else you must give me,' Terril said.

'Anything.'

'You must give me the gun, Don Antonio. The Winchester.'

9

Searching

He rested at the hacienda for three days, regaining his strength, eating well, forming his plans. Apart from one short visit to Josefina's grave, he remained indoors, hidden, knowing that the slightest whisper of his presence to the outside world could have men seeking him. Texas was awash with greed. There were many bounty hunters: unscrupulous men who would turn him in, or even gun him down, for the chance of a quick buck. But nobody came looking for him and, once again, moving by night, he bade his farewells to his patron. With the horse of his choice, Fedora, fresh supplies and clothing, he rode out into the darkness, having scant knowledge of where he was headed, but with the desire to track his enemy down burning inside him like a white-hot iron.

Constantly he wondered whether Florencia was still alive. He had heard that the Comanche, who bitterly resented white encroachment, delighted in taking female captives to boost their low birthrate. It might be as well if she was dead; if so, he hoped she had found peace with her sister, the victim of the same evil monster. Florencia's young life had been a pampered one, but now she would have been faced with the most appalling experience. He did not know what to hope for. Whatever had happened, Aimijo must be found and destroyed.

Don Antonio had made mention of the Staked Plains, the wild country in the Panhandle, north of the Red River. He wondered how deeply the Texas Rangers had probed in their search. He wished he could have discussed matters with them, have formulated some sort of plan. But the only assistance they would offer him would be in the form of leg-shackles.

For days he rode north, following the river, seeing the terrain stretch to far horizons, broken here and there by creeks margined by willowy cotton-woods. The weather was tinged by the foretaste of winter. He lived off the land, avoiding human contact. He was no stranger to living 'wild', enjoying the patient company of Fedora. He encoun-tered an abundance of natural life, dark-coloured wild turkeys with bronze incandescence, burros, bandit coatis foraging for carrion, coyotes, jack-rabbits, cottontail deer and once a bear.

Sooner or later, he knew, he would have to establish contact with humans. He would have to start asking ques-tions.

One morning he slept late in his bedroll and was aroused by gunfire. He sat up, reaching for the Winchester which he kept close. He rose to his feet, creeping towards the edge of the cottonwoods, drawn by the sound. Before him, a plain stretched and across it was a large buffalo herd, showing dense and umber against the lush ground. A distant puff of smoke and the boom of heavy-calibered rifles indicated the presence of hunters. Buffalo hides were now an attractive commercial commodity, being used, amongst other things, for leather. Animals were being slain by the thousands. Today was no exception. Soon the ground became a carpet of shaggy carcasses; many animals threshed in their death-throes. Presently the shooting trailed off, and men moved amongst the buffalo, skinning them where they had fallen, their knives flashing in the sunlight.

Terril realized that now might be a good time to re-establish his links with white people. He urged the reluctant Fedora through the carcasses, feeling as if the eyes of the beasts were staring at him, reproaching all mankind for what had happened. Overhead the scavenger birds were darkening the sky. Fifteen minutes later he was drinking coffee from a tin cup at the buffalo hunters' camp-fire. They were a rum crowd, some of them beginning to look like the buffalo they hunted, filthy, itching with mange. Many were smeared with blood. The sweet, sickish stench of slaughter hung about them. Some individuals boasted that they had shot over a hundred animals. They were so exultant with their success that they showed no inquisitiveness towards Terril, but he learned that they had recently had contact with a small breakaway band of Indians camped some five miles to the north. This band, Comanches under a chief called Owl, had declared that they wished to surrender to the white man and thus avoid trouble.

Meanwhile, apparently, there was a big gathering of Indians in the country. A chief called Quanah Parker was attracting support, not only from his own Comanche people, but from Cheyenne, Kiowa and Arapahoe tribesmen. Quanah Parker had called a council and he had prophesied that an all-out attack would drive the white men out. The Comanches believed that they had the medicine to turn the white man's bullets away.

Terril tentatively mentioned that he was seeking a Mexican with a young woman, but his companions shook their heads, knowing nothing . . . or fearing to tell. How could he be sure?

He returned to his own camp, watching how winged scavengers came to pick at the remains left. The pelts had been taken. The whole thing sickened Terril. How long could the herds sustain this mass killing? No wonder the Indians resented it.

Next morning he was on the move early, feeling that he now had somewhere to aim for. The Comanches the hunters had mentioned, hopefully wanting only peace with the white-eyes, might have some information concerning the whereabouts of his quarry. But being in Indian country was dangerous and he travelled warily. Ambush would be easy and he had many enemies. He kept clear of open country as much as possible, seeking cover through forests. In the afternoon he topped a high mesa of sheer red cliffs. Beneath him was a twisting river. Straddling its banks was a small Indian village, smoke rising from the vents of a dozen conical tepees, all painted with designs and showing white in the sun. Even at distance he could hear the yap of dogs and the cries of children. Ponies were grazing along the far bank. This was clearly not a camp of Indians preparing for war, so taking a calculated risk he rode openly down towards it.

A boy, tending some ponies, was the first to see him, and he ran back to the tepees, shouting. Within a minute Terril knew he was being observed. Keeping his hands well clear of his weapons, he nudged Fedora down into the camp, passing through the tepees, trailed by yapping dogs until he reached a central point where a large fire blazed. The dogs trailed off and he was confronted by several warriors. All were clad in hunting-shirts and leggings. Some of them had coloured their scalps with vermilion. Others had queues of horse-hair suspended from their heads, reaching almost to the ground. One man stood out from the others, obviously the chief, and Terril knew instinctively that this was Owl. He wore buffalo-hide leggings and a Bowie knife hung from his belt. He was white-haired, his face weather-seamed and weary, his nose aquiline.

Terril dismounted, making the palm-out sign of peace.

Owl motioned him to join them around the fire, and a pipe was filled and passed along. Terril took his turn, puffing until his face was wreathed in smoke, observing the Indian practice of dragging the whole operation out as long as possible. He remained alert, watching around him, hoping against hope that Florencia might suddenly appear. True enough, some young people stood around peering at him, but they all appeared true-blood Comanche with feathers in their hair.

Owl did not speak English, but another warrior, at his elbow, translated what was said.

Terril took his time getting to the point of his visit, allowing Owl to ramble on about how trouble was brewing, how soon there would be a big fight. Quanah Parker claimed to have received a vision from *Tai-me* foretelling a mighty victory. But Owl emphasized that he was tired of fighting soldiers, that he wanted to take his people along the path of peace and live on a reservation.

Only when he had had his full say, did Terril mention that he was seeking a Mexican called Armijo who might have a young woman with him.

Owl's expression betrayed nothing. He continued to draw on his pipe and presently, with the evening growing cool, a woman brought him a blanket for his shoulders. Through the interpreter, Terril pressed him for an answer.

'If I tell you of this man,' Owl said, 'will you tell the white soldiers that Owl means no harm, that he wants only peace for his people?'

Terril's pulse had begun to race. He said: 'I will tell the soldiers that your heart is good.' He knew that the soldiers would care little for anything an escaped convict might say, but Owl obviously imagined him to have some influence.

'And there is something else,' Owl went on. 'The gun you have, the one that shoots many bullets without reloading.'

Terril glanced at the Winchester he had placed on the ground beside him. It was his safeguard in this wilderness. Added to which, he had brought the weapon with the express wish of using it to destroy his enemy. He had no wish to give it up.

'If Owl wants only peace, why does he want this gun?' he asked. The chief did not hesitate.

'Gun will bring many suppers. It would be a good trade for the information you want,' Owl said.

Presently, Terril lifted the weapon and gave it to him.

The old man grunted with pleasure, examining the gun, opening the chamber, fingering the bullets. After a long time, he placed the weapon at his side, patting it possessively, a cryptic smile creasing his face as if he was congratulating himself on his prize.

'The man you seek is with Quanah Parker,' he said.

Terril nodded with satisfaction.

'And the woman?'

Owl shook his head. 'I do not know of the woman.'

10

Massacre

Terril spent the night with the Comanches, spreading his bedroll in the lodge of Chief Owl. He guessed it was not in the Indians' interest to harm him whilst they hoped to go into the reservation. Come another day and the wind might change and they would be glad enough to take up the war trail with Quanah Parker. Next morning, with the first glaze of frost cloaking the autumn grasses, he saddled Fedora and rode out. He regretted surrendering the gun, for it had seemed the very core of his mission and he was now reduced in weaponry to the percussion pistol, and his knife. Neither of which were ideal for hunting. But he had survived many a day in the wilderness with less, and he would do so again.

He headed north. The country was awe-inspiring: cactus-dotted sandhills with a rim of high peaks stretched away to the north. The dips and swells in the ground provided ample hiding-places for anybody who wished to ambush him. He kept his revolver charged and ready. He remembered how well it had served him when first he'd come to Texas all those years back. If only he could have foreseen events; if only he could have changed things around.

Chief Owl had mentioned that Quanah Parker was camped near the junction of Elk Creek with the Red River — that was where the big sun-dance had been held. He knew that all large Indian camps had their share of renegade whites trailing along — unscrupulous traders, Mexican and Anglos, called comancheros. Big money was to be made trading guns to the Indians, and Terril was pinning his hopes on Armijo and, please God, the girl being amongst them. He had now concluded that he did not want

Florencia to be dead. He wanted her alive. He wanted to rescue her, destroy her tormentor, and take her home. Even if he was then returned to prison, he would at least have accomplished something and brought some compensation to Don Antonio for the awful events he had brought to the family. The fault had not been his, never had been, but his mere presence had brought with it the awful tragedy of murder, kidnap and grief.

The land stretched far northeastward, populated occasionally by ranchers and settlers. They were hardy folk, who kept themselves well fortified, some saying that they would sooner burn their homes down than leave them to the Indians. This was the sort of stubbornness that could end in tragedy. Terril had little idea of how long it would take him to reach Quanah's camp, but now he was drawn to it like a pin to a magnet. Owl might have been lying to him, might only have been interested in gaining possession of the gun, but Terril discounted the idea. The prospect of Armijo's being with Quanah Parker was all he had to go on; if it proved a fruitless mission, then he would have to turn his attention elsewhere, but he would keep going just as long as it took, just as long as he was spared to continue the hunt.

But all his planning and scheming went awry the next morning. He was awakened by the sound of a gun's hammer being thumbed back. He cursed as he raised his head and saw that some dozen or so heavily armed men were trampling in about him. No doubt they'd spotted the grazing Fedora and come to investigate.

He went numb with frustration as he realized that these men were Texas Rangers.

He sat up in his bedroll. He could see that they posed no immediate threat, for soon guns were slipped back into holsters.

One of them, a big man with yellow hair and wearing a red coat, extended his hand which Terril shook. 'Captain Jack Colpett,' he explained. 'Frontier Battalion of Texas Rangers, out from Fort Sill. Where you headed, mister?'

Terril saw no point in tying himself in knots with lies, but he needed to be economical with the truth. 'I'm headed for Quanah Parker's camp on Elk Creek,' he said. 'I'm looking for the daughter of Don Antonio Baltran. She's been kidnapped.'

Colpett nodded his shaggy head. 'I know about that,' he said, accepting a cigar from a companion. He bit the end off. 'You won't get near Quanah's camp, though. The country's swarming with Indians, and they sure don't make strangers welcome.'

One of the Rangers, a narrow-faced man, had been staring at Terril in a way that made him uneasy. Suddenly the man spoke his mind.

'Knew I seen you some place before,' he said. 'It's just come to me. You was on trial for murder up at San Antonio. I was on the jury that convicted you.'

Terril felt the blood drain from his face. He started to shake his head in denial, but he knew it was hopeless.

'Figured you'd been locked away for life,' the narrow-faced Ranger commented, matter of fact.

Terril glanced about, sickened, desperate thoughts of escape pounding through his brain. They surrounded him, armed to the teeth. One step of flight, and he'd be riddled with bullets.

'Better chain him up,' Colpett said, lighting his cigar.

★   ★   ★

If Terril suspected that he would immediately be escorted back to prison, he was wrong. There were a dozen Rangers in this troop, all armed with carbines and Walker Colts. Gradually some of their names became known to Terril: Webster, Fulton, Edison, Rawson, McDowell, Carao. They had earned a nickname from the Mexicans: *Los Tejanos Sanguinarios* — the

Bloodthirsty Texans. These men had not ventured into hostile country in pursuit of an escaped convict. They had bigger fish to fry. Terril was relieved of his weapons, placed astride Fedora with his legs linked by chain beneath the animal's belly, and the journey northward was recommenced. He was fed when a stop was made, and escorted for bodily functions. He was in the particular care of a Ranger called Amos Kelly, a baccy-chewing, diligent man, who kept the key to Terril's chains on a string around his neck. When Terril was on foot his legs were linked on a short section of chain and he was allowed not the slightest chance of escape. He was clearly a burden to these men, but they did not shirk their duty.

Kelly was not unfriendly. At one stop he took out a photograph of his wife and daughter and proudly showed them to Terril. His captors generally remained on constant alert, scanning the surrounding terrain for sign of hostile Indians, posting guards at each stop. These men lived by the hard code of survival.

Captain Colpett was cheerful, a good leader, and he showed no malice towards Terril. In fact he was quite talkative when they halted that evening and made camp. After ensuring that the guards were set to his liking, he sat with Terril and explained the purpose of his mission.

'We're headed up to a place called Adobe Walls,' he said. 'There's about thirty folks up there, mostly buffalo hunters, and at least one woman. We're gonna escort them out, otherwise Quanah will massacre the lot.'

'Do you know anything of Diego Armijo and the girl he kidnapped?' Terril enquired.

'Sure, we know about them.' Colpett nodded. 'We heard Armijo is running guns to the Comanche and if we can find him and destroy him, it will be a blow well struck.'

'And the girl, Florencia Baldran?'

Colpett took a sip of coffee. 'We

know no more than you do. She may be dead, who can tell? But our main task is to rescue them folk from Adobe Walls. We're up against thousands of Comanches, with scores of Arapahoes and Cheyennes thrown in. Quanah's got 'em stirred up to fever-pitch. Once we get to Adobe Walls we'll round those folk up and get out as quick as we can.'

Terril nodded. He felt totally frustrated, but thankful that at least he was being taken in the right direction. Maybe he would stand some chance of breaking free up at Adobe Walls. But right now he could not see how.

During the next three days the atmosphere of constant vigilance was as tight as a bowstring. At night, Terril lay gazing up at a sky cluttered with cold stars, recalling how, on the night of his wedding, he and Josefina had gazed aloft and pondered on the heaven awaiting them.

The temperature had dropped. A ripe wind blew from the north. Winter was in the making and each morning they awoke expecting to find the ground carpeted with snow, but none came.

They traversed country that was split by deep ridges, groves of trees and sluggish rivers. They stopped at several homesteads, where the residents were forted up and anxiously watching the surrounding hills for sign of Indians. Colpett told them to make ready by the time he returned, that they would then be escorted away from Indian country. Some said they would be staying put, others said they would be gone by the time the Rangers returned, others agreed to take up his offer. But they all concurred on one thing: Quanah was mighty bad medicine.

He slept well on his last night of captivity in the hands of the Rangers, despite the discomfort his chains brought. At dawn he was bludgeoned to wakefulness by the crash of guns and shouts of men. Aware of impending danger, he rolled out of his blanket into some thick brush, conscious of men rushing about him. Suddenly, directly in front of him, he saw one of the Rangers struggling with a feather-bedecked Indian who was raising a hunting-knife. When it plunged down-ward, Terril heard the awful suck of steel into flesh, and the Ranger fell away, blood pumping from the jagged slash in his chest. The air was filled with terrorizing whoops and yells. More shots were thundering, more shouts. Terril realized that, despite their wari-ness, the Rangers had been caught by a dawn attack, and there was nothing he could do, being chained, but wait for whatever fate had in store.

Colpett was backing towards him, blasting away with his Walker Colt, then he let out a weird gurgling sound. As he twisted Terril could see that an arrow had gone through his neck. He dropped, and immediately a painted warrior was kneeling upon him, slicing his scalp away with deft cuts of his knife.

There seemed to be ever increasing numbers of Indians, overwhelming

Rangers in sudden scurries of violence. Gradually the gunfire dwindled to be replaced by the exultant cries of the Comanches.

Lying half-concealed by leaves, Terril shrank to his smallest size, praying that he might go unnoticed. The smell of sweat and blood were all around. Indians were crouched over prostrate Rangers, men who only hours earlier had been the companions of Terril — now they had been slaughtered, and for some reason he could not understand, he had survived, but for how long?

11

Captive

Suddenly an Indian glanced in his direction, looked away, and then his surprised eyes returned. He pointed, jabbering in his own tongue. Attention was immediately focused on Terril, and he suspected that his death was imminent. They grouped around him like panting wolves surrounding the kill. He was helpless, having no words left to plead for mercy. Just get it over quickly, he thought. In expectation, he clenched his eyes shut, hoping that his dispatch would be quick. He smelt the closeness of an Indian, felt fingers grasp his hair and pull his head back, exposing his throat as if for cutting. He prepared himself for the sharp pain of the blade across his throat, the gasp and bloody choke, the encroaching oblivion — but for a moment the greatest pain he felt came from the cruel grip of fingers in his hair.

The voice came, thick with Mexican accent, thick with the slur of liquor. 'Leave him!'

For a moment, there was hesitation, then the slackening of the grip on his hair. The Indian, so close to slaying him, cursed, his blade poised in mid-air, then Terril felt himself tossed aside like a useless rag-doll.

He lay upon the ground and only then did he dare open his eyes. He saw boots, Spanish-type boots inlaid with a fancy pattern. The Mexican voice came again. 'A prisoner of the Rangers, eh? Are you one of Armijo's traders?'

Still not raising his head, Terril forced his lips into forming words. '*Si*, I have business with Armijo.'

His companion laughed mockingly and said, 'Well, *amigo*, you best be telling the truth, otherwise Armijo will hand you back to the Indians and they will have fun with you. They are not kind to Anglos.'

Only now did Terril look up. He saw a swarthy man in a sombrero peering at him — obviously a comanchero, a man who made his living trading guns to the Comanches so that they could kill white men. He was wearing two cross-belted pistols. Significant was the fact that he was an associate of Diego Armijo and he intended to deliver Terril directly to him.

'Stand up, *amigo*,' his apparent saviour said. 'Don't grovel like a dog!'

Terril stirred his stiffened limbs into life, struggling with the awkwardness of his chains and levering himself to his feet. Around him was a scene of horror. The bodies of the Rangers lay all about, bloodied. Familiar faces now showed the ghastly record of scalping, for the skin lay slack upon the bones, masks of grisly death, and their corpses were punctured by a multitude of arrow and bullet wounds. Indians were plundering from the campsite anything of value they could find — buffalo skins, blankets, weapons, culinary utensils. Then they turned their attention back to the bodies, cutting and hacking at them, chopping away limbs, disembowelling them. Colpett's tongue was drawn out, a sharp stick placed through it.

Terril tried to focus his attention on his own dire circumstances. At least he had survived — but at what cost? What grim fate awaited him? Once Armijo discovered his true identity he would delight in subjecting him to the cruellest suffering. But now his eyes seized on the sprawled, naked body of Amos Kelly, the Ranger formerly entrusted with the special care of the prisoner. His bloody garments had been cast beside him in a heap.

'The keys,' Terril gasped, holding up his shackles. 'They are in his pocket. You must release me.'

The Mexican nodded as if springing to obey an order. He stepped across to the clothing, rummaged in the pockets and held up the keys.

'Release me,' Terril repeated.

The Mexican grinned. 'We will leave that pleasure for Armijo,' he said.

The Indians had now finished their task of ransacking the dead. They were pleased with their haul of Walker Colts, carbines and ammunition. Even more pleased with the fresh scalps that dangled from their belts. The human remains would be left to coyotes, wolves and buzzards. The denizens of the wild were doing well of late. Horses had been rounded up; Terril noticed that Fedora was among them. The Indians also had ponies of their own, and the whole party swung on to their backs — all except for Terril. He was afforded no such luxury.

One shackle linking his ankles was unfastened, leaving the chain dragging. He was thus able to take a lengthier stride. A strip of buffalo hide was fixed around his neck and he was pulled along like a leashed dog by the Mexican. The latter cursed and struck out at him each time he stumbled.

Sometimes warriors rushed at him, waving their tomahawks, their faces fearful, as if they were about to kill him, but they always held back at the last moment, pointing their fingers at him in derision.

The party travelled briskly through the morning, herding the horses with impatience, pausing only briefly for water at the streams they encountered. Terril struggled along, gasping for air. His tortured mind did not wrestle with the uncertainties of the future; he was too busy ensuring that his next step was accomplished. But inside him was a weird emotion. Each yard of traversed ground brought him closer to the man he had hunted these past years, the man he had dreamed of destroying. Now he was in the unenviable position of being a chained captive, soon to be, in all probability, at the mercy of the man he had hunted. The roles were reversed in the most alarming fashion, and somehow he was going to have to turn the tables. But how? He cursed the chains that handicapped him. There seemed little likelihood of Amos Kelly's keys being put to good use in the immediate future.

He groaned and struggled on, concentrating on the rumps of the horses in whose dung he stumbled, sucking up water when he was given the opportunity, not conversing with either his Mexican temporary saviour or his red-skinned associates. He took some slight comfort: at least he was alive, and as such he had hope of achieving something.

And then at last an exultation was cutting through the Indians and he sensed that they were nearing their homecoming. Sure enough, as they skirted the sharp backbone of a ridge and swung round into a broad valley a vast village was revealed — dozens of tepees, spread wide, smoke rising from many cooking-fires; he could hear excited cries of children, yapping of dogs, shouts of women. Numerous frames stood between the lodges; from these, red meat hung. Considerable areas were devoted to pegged-out buffalo hides, drying in the sun.

And Terril knew that they had reached the great encampment of the legendary Quanah Parker — nemesis and scourge of the white man.

As the party rode in swarms of Indians surrounded them in a suffocating throng, all pushing forward to peer at the captive. Terril glanced around, his tortured mind hoping, praying, that he might get sight of Florencia Baltran. But if ever there was a case of seeking a needle in a haystack, this was it.

And it seemed to Terril, that he had come to an earthly Hades.

12

Torture

'Who are you?'

The words pierced through his semi-consciousness. He forced his eyes open, then, blinded by light, he closed them again. A boot thudded into his ribs, causing him to jerk like a puppet on a string.

'Who are you?' Now the voice was quickened by impatience.

Terril groaned. Then he opened his eyes again and this time they stayed open. A cruel Mexican face loomed over him. Bearded, heavily moustached; gold teeth; the eyes fierce. And it occurred to him that there was a familiarity in it. His swimming senses solidified around the fact, and associated with it a death — death of . . . Armijo, the man he had shot. The

Mexican gazing at him had similar features because he was his brother. Here was the man who had murdered Terril's wife, nigh killed him, had kidnapped Florencia Baltran and committed terrible acts of criminality. He was Diego Armijo.

Terril groaned with anger and frustration, strained against the chains that still shackled his wrists and had been reattached to his ankles. He was fastened to a stake that had been driven into the ground, deep in the very heart of the Comanche village.

He was dimly aware that there was a number of women and children watching at a distance.

'Where is Florencia?' he gasped.

A look of puzzlement spread across Armijo's arrogant features. The two men had never faced each other before, apart from once on a dark night, across the barrel of a gun. Terril realized that Armijo did not know him from Adam.

'You have been sent by Don Antonio?' the Mexican demanded.

Terril said nothing.

Armijo lost his patience. He spat at Terril, who felt the spittle running down his cheek. 'I do not know you,' Armijo snarled. 'I do not want you. You are nothing to me. I will give you to the Comanche women. They will enjoy hacking your manhood off. They enjoy playing with a white-eye, seeing him die in agony.'

He drove his boot into Terril's side in a cruel kick, then he turned and strode off. Pain was throbbing through Terril. He suspected his ribs were cracked.

He was in misery, plunging deep into his pit of despair. He was starving, but he gave little thought to food for it was water he craved. His throat felt like sandpaper and his lips were cracked and bleeding. He strained against the stake securing him, strained against his chains, but found not a fraction of give. After all his searching, all his years of dreaming of vengeance, he had at last found his prey, only to be denied inflicting the retribution the Mexican so completely deserved. He had not even been able to speak his mind, to speak the words of damnation that he yearned to pour into Armijo's ears. Such would have brought his immediate demise. At present, Armijo considered him worthless, not even worth the effort of killing.

His mind tortured by his terrible predicament, Terril lapsed into and out of consciousness. In his brain he saw again the awful images of the massacres of his Ranger companions. They had obviously been taken by complete surprise, the throats of Colpett's guards slashed before they could have considered raising any alarm.

God only knew where the key to his chains was now. He had not seen the man who held the key since the arrival at the village. He might well have discarded the key; he might even have travelled on elsewhere. Terril groaned. Before final merciful death claimed him, he sensed he would die a thousand lesser deaths.

During his periods of awareness

Terril felt the intense cold. Winter had at last arrived in earnest, snow falling about him, coating him, freezing him. His teeth began to chatter. He cast his eyes around again realizing that he was in a cleared space in the centre of the village. He could see the tepees surrounding him, some of them showing the glow of internal fires and the smoke rising into the snow-thick air from their vents. He licked his lips. There would be water there and food and warmth.

He could hear occasional voices, the shrill voices of women, the cries of children, the clink of cooking-pots, the barking of dogs — and he could smell the odour that seemed to hang about all Indians. But it all seemed distant and he began to imagine that he was no longer of any interest to anybody, that he might be left here to starve to death, chained to this damn pole. But it was not so.

It was evening when the women came for him, their cruel hands seizing hold of him like claws, their voices raised in cackling shrieks. They had lit a fire close by, the flames were now leaping high, painting their faces in hideous, flickering orange. In the nightmare light, he also glimpsed the knives they held and a tremor shook him. He knew that the greater the fear he showed, the greater his suffering would be. He gritted his teeth together, shut his eyes and knew he had no option but to submit to whatever horror they had in store for him.

They had no intention of releasing him from the pole. They clearly had no means of doing so apart from cutting the pole down or pulling it from the ground and that was not part of their plan.

He was sprawled on his back, the weight of women pinning him to the ground. Behind his tormentors he glimpsed a pack of dogs, their tongues lolled, waiting in the expectation that soon there would be blood for them to lap. He was conscious that his clothes were being cut away, that he was being reduced to nakedness so that he could feel the sharp sting of snow touching him. Sharp nails scratched him, cruel fingers poked and prodded him bringing gales of laughter from his tormentors. He felt stifled as they pressed upon him. Now, completely divested of any clothing, he felt the sharpness of knives criss-crossing his bare chest. He had heard of the death of a thousand cuts. Was this to be his fate? Almost in rhythm with the pain of the cuts, a drum was being beaten . . . the cuts became regular. He could feel the warmth of blood coursing over him.

He prayed for unconsciousness, for blessed oblivion, but it would not come and his pain became so intense, he screamed out.

The male voice came without an emotion, speaking rapidly in Comanche, but there was an insistence about it that brought howls of indignation from the women. At first the voice brought no other reaction. It came again, sterner. Now it was a demand. He felt the weight of the women being withdrawn from him, their grumblings indicating the frustration they felt.

The voice spat out one final command. He could hear the pad of feet in the snow, departing feet. The women were leaving him — and Terril knew that, for some crazy reason beyond his understanding, he had been spared, at least for the moment. But he had been hurt — hurt badly. He could feel the blood on his entire body. Seeping from a myriad of cuts, draining the strength, the life, from him. Now, at last, his consciousness wavered. He groaned. His senses deserted him.

13

Escape

Why am I alive?

He was lying on his back upon something soft. Above him, he could see the vent of a tepee, the criss-cross of cedar poles thrust through it, and beyond that the smoke-hazed blueness of sky. He was aware of warmth, coming from his left and, turning his head, he could see a fire crackling with logs. He was inside a tepee that was decorated with elkskin hangings, a blanket over him. He moved his arm, wincing at the pain it caused — but he became aware of something else. His shackles had been removed.

His mind grappled with gruesome recollections. He had visions of evil faces, of shrieking voices, of slow death beckoning him. And yet he was here, away from pestering hands, criss-crossing knives torturing his naked flesh. Why?

He had no answers. It took energy to seek them. He had no energy. He needed relief from his pain. He slept.

John Terril was awakened by a soothing touch. He gazed up into eyes that he had seen before — female, green eyes. He tried to speak, but his words ended in a choke. The woman was kneeling beside him, leaning over him. She was young. She was wearing a bright calico shirt and a tin head band, scalloped at the upper edge like a crown. Her hair was blacker than the feathers of a crow. She had a bowl and cloth, and had been washing the clotted blood away from the cuts on his chest.

She reached to one side and lifted a gourd to his lips.

Water flowed into his parched mouth. No wine had ever tasted sweeter.

As she put the gourd aside his speech came, but his brain could not keep pace with his words. 'You are . . . ?'

'Florencia,' she said. 'You must rest. It is best you do not speak.'

He gasped as realization took hold of him. *Florencia* . . .

'But . . . '

'I was kidnapped by Diego Armijo,' she told him, soothing some sort of balm into his cuts. Her touch had the gentleness of butterfly wings. 'It was terrible what they did to Maria, my servant. But she escaped.'

'I know,' Terril murmured.

'Armijo brought me here,' she continued. 'He sold me to the Comanches. At first I was very frightened, but they have been good to me, and the son of Quanah, White Parker, has made me his wife. I love him. I want to stay with him. He is called *el Bueno* — the Good Man. I think we have made a baby together.'

Terril gasped, the implications gradually seeping into his jaded mind. He could scarcely believe what he was hearing.

'But your father,' he said. 'He is crazy with worry.'

She worked steadily; she required him to sit up while she slipped a bandage around his chest and shoulders.

'I am very sad for my father,' she said. 'I have no way of getting word to him, to tell him that he need not worry. White Parker has said he will find a way to get a message to him, but now is not a good time. The Comanches are sick of being pushed back, of their land being stolen, of the buffalo being exterminated. Soon there will be none left and the people will starve. The whites do not realize how bad it is for the Indians.'

'You have met your father-in-law?' he enquired. 'Quanah.'

'Sí. He has had a vision. He believes he can drive the white-eyes away, that the old ways will return.'

'He is here? At this camp?'

She bobbed her dark head. She looked immensely pretty, so reminiscent of her sister. She said: 'He is forming a big war-party. Armijo will supply him with many guns in exchange for buffalo hides. Soon they will ride out and fight the white-eye.'

For a moment he remained silent. There seemed so much to take in, so much that had come as a total surprise. His thoughts swung to the man he hated above all others. 'Armijo does not know who I am,' he said. 'If he finds out, nothing will stop him from killing me.'

'I know. That is why you must stay here and rest. Keep away from him. If you try to escape, they will cut the tendons of your legs.'

Presently he asked; 'Why did the women let me go? Why did they not kill me?'

'I spoke with my husband. He does the things I ask.'

'And you asked that I be spared.'

Again she bobbed her head. 'And he got the key for your chains.'

He did not express his gratitude in words. He reached out and rested his hand on hers. He owed her much.

She adjusted a pillow for him to lay his head upon. 'I will get you some food. You must rest.'

He leaned back.

When he presently slept, having taken some thick broth, his dreams were sweeter.

★　★　★

Quanah spoke better English than many Americans whom Terril had known. Fastened into his black hair were feathers dyed in all colours of the rainbow. His hair hung in long braids. Florencia had told him how Quanah's mother, Cynthia Parker, a white woman, had been taken prisoner by the Comanches, had adapted to the Indian way of life, and become the wife of a noted war-chief of the Nacone band, Peta Nacone. But Nacone had been killed by Texas Rangers, Cynthia captured by the whites and thrown into prison. Quanah, now an orphan, had taken refuge with the Quahadi band and subsequently became their leader. In recent years he and his warlike tribesmen had held the territory in a grip of terror, waging war on the buffalo hunters whom they considered were destroying their way of life.

Now the chief sat beside Terril as he continued his recovery. He was chewing on peyote. His eyes were hooded, mysterious, and occasionally he belched.

'Why were the Rangers holding you prisoner?' he asked.

Terril saw no point in lying. 'Because I escaped from a prison. I had been put there because I killed a man.'

'If every man was locked up because he killed somebody, we would all be in prison.'

Terril nodded. He could hardly believe the most feared Indian on the Texas plains was conversing with him.

'You have been hurt badly,' Quanah said. 'You are lucky to be alive. It was because Florencia wanted you to live.'

'I am grateful to her,' Terril said. 'I

am glad she is happy here. She has a good husband. But her father does not know what has happened to her. He grieves for her.'

Quanah indicated his understanding. 'After I have killed all white-eyes in Comancheria, I will get word to him. I think his daughter will produce good Comanche babies. I have many wives, but they do not make enough babies.'

He left Terril then, left him with his thoughts.

★　★　★

Terril lived with the Comanches through that winter, seeing how their numbers were gradually supplemented by the arrival of Cheyenne and Kiowa warriors. All were anxious to take part in the destruction of the white men that Quanah had promised.

Terril's body had healed, though he would bear the scars for the rest of his days, however long that might be. He lived with the family of Ten Bears and was generally treated kindly by the same women who would have tortured him to death. Things had changed. Quanah had said he was not to be harmed, unless he violated the hospitality shown. All this, Terril knew, was because Quanah favoured his son's wife, Florencia. He was accommodated in the Indian way, feeding from the great pot of stew kept constantly simmering in the centre of the tepee. But he was never allowed to forget that he was not Comanche, that his status was somewhere close to that of a dog.

He was to work. He laboured with the squaws, pegging out the skins of buffalo while they dried, using sharp bone scrapers to remove flesh, gathering buffalo chips for the cooking-fires, chopping kindling, washing cooking-utensils in the rivers. The women would chastize and tease him, but he was spared the details of such because everything was spoken in the Comanche tongue.

He saw Florencia every day, and she

passed onto him what news she had. That the bluecoats had ventured into Comancheria as if preparing for the big fight that was to come.

Sometimes he would accompany the hunters, and they would find the big buffalo herds and slaughter them with lance and arrow. The carcasses were put to good use — the meat salted away, the blood drunk to give strength, the bones, horns and hoofs were made into spoons and utensils. Sinews were used as bow strings.

The skins were removed in huge quantities, and cured by trampling the skin. More and more tepees were set aside for storage, and when Terril enquired as to why so many skins were being stored, he was told, quite candidly, to trade for guns.

At first he moved about the camp warily, fearful lest he should encounter Armijo, for he knew that now was not the time to confront him. But Armijo was absent, and he eventually learned that the Mexican was far to the south, finding the guns that would enable the Indians to fight the white-eyes.

But Terril knew that he was living in a limbo. He could not remain here for ever, and he became well aware that the Indians considered him an unnecessary burden, suffered only to humour Quanah. His every thought dwelt on escape. He had wondered whether, if he got away, Florencia would suffer on account of it? But he eventually concluded that she would not. She had gone true Comanche and was entirely accepted as one of them. On the other hand, *his* presence was only tolerated; any attempt at escape would give them an excuse to kill him, but it was a chance he had to take. Furthermore, he had a duty to attempt to reach Don Antonio with the news of his daughter's survival.

One night in late spring he rose from his buffalo mattress, aware that everybody else in the tepee was asleep. He reckoned it was well after midnight. The embers of the cooking-fire had burned low, and the flap was open to let cool air and a sheen of moonlight in. He gathered up the few necessities he had prepared during the day, including cold jerky and some corn-meal, and on tiptoe he left the tepee. He knew that his absence would not immediately arouse suspicion, for calls of nature were not unusual.

But as he ghosted through the silent camp, dark shadows loomed about him and a snarling arose and he glimpsed the whiteness of teeth in the gloom. He suspected that if he proceeded further the dogs might tear into him and any attempt at stealth would be useless. He was now aware that other dogs, from further afield, were growling. To his horror, he heard drowsy voices calling out from the adjacent tepees, male and female, shouting at the dogs to be quiet. He stood motionless, recalling how Florencia had once told him that if he attempted escape and was caught, he would have the tendons of his legs severed to prevent any recurrence.

Which would be worse? That or death?

For what seemed a lifetime he waited. At last the dogs lost interest. Only then did he return to his mattress — like a dog himself, with his tail between his legs. He would try again tomorrow night.

Tomorrow night came — but once more he aroused the dogs with the same frightening results.

It was at the third attempt that he reached the fringe of the camp and realized that he had eluded the canines. He immediately broke into a run, carrying the burden of supplies he had brought. He kept going, his legs pumping rhythmically, until his lungs were bursting. Dawn found him well clear of the village.

He wondered whether he was already being pursued. As the light grew stronger he repeatedly looked back, but the terrain appeared devoid of life.

A plan was forming in his mind, but he would need all the luck on God's earth to achieve it. He must make the most of the time he had been given.

He travelled for another day, covering as much ground as he could. He moved through land that was green with spring, flowering with willows, cotton-woods, hackberry and chinaberry. Next morning he heard gunfire and when he reached a wide, saucer-like expanse of prairie, his eyes were greeted with the familiar sight of white hunters firing on a buffalo herd. Soon, he made his presence known. Realizing that he looked more Indian than white, he approached with the utmost caution, holding his hands high and calling out: 'I am a white man!'

As startled gazes swung in his direction, he reinforced his first mes-sage. 'I have escaped from the Indians!'

Cautious hunters gestured him to come closer, all the while expecting some Indian trick, but eventually guns were lowered and they beckoned him in, pre-pared to listen to what he had to say.

Tales of escape from the Indians were not unusual and before long he had their trust. He learned that they were men from the hunters' settlement at Adobe Walls — a half-day's journey away. He recalled that the Texas Rangers had been on their way to evacuate these hunters out of the country because of the Indian threat. The worst expectations had not yet been realized. It was the Rangers who had paid the penalty. But Terril had seen enough to know that it was only a matter of time before wholesale massacre occurred. As soon as Quanah got his guns the territory would run red with blood — and Adobe Walls was in an exposed position.

That evening, the party loaded up its wagons with the valuable hides and started back towards Adobe Walls, leaving the prairie dotted with the obscene, pink hulks of stripped buffalo carcasses. Terril prayed that his escape had not brought trouble to Florencia. She was a good person and Terril regretted most profoundly that she had embraced the Indian way of life.

14

The Raid

Adobe Walls was a fledgling settlement built around the ruins of an earlier trading post. It stood close to East Adobe Creek, near the main migratory trail of the buffalo, its primary purpose to make money out of the 200 or so hunters who worked the area. There was a storehouse, set up by two merchants, Myers and Leonard, and a picket corral. Two more small sod houses stood to the south. Next to those were the blacksmith's shop, a restaurant and the spacious sod-walled saloon, run by an Irishman called Hanrahan, who stocked plenty of red-eye whiskey. The saloon had an earthen roof which was held up by a large ridgepole. All of these structures doubled up as lodging-places for those in residence, both shifting and permanent. Most of the buildings had two-foot-thick walls and were well fortified, but in view of the sheer numbers of Indians in the vicinity, nowhere was safe.

When John Terril and the hunters rode into the settlement there was a total of some thirty persons present, including a woman. Terril immediately took advantage of the facilities on offer, feeding well and taking a long rest in Hanrahan's saloon. Here, the bar consisted of a huge log sunk into the dirt floor, its top smoothed with an axe.

On awakening, Terril dwelt more and more on the plan that had occurred to him.

The Texas Rangers had foreseen the danger that this place was in, and had they not been destroyed themselves, might well have arranged the evacuation of the community until the Indians had been quelled. Terril knew that once Quanah had the rifles that Diego Armijo was supplying, Adobe Walls

would be the first target for his rampant
hordes.

* * *

'It'd be a risky business,' Billy Dixon
said, stuffing tobacco into his pipe. It
gurgled as he drew on it. He was a tall
and lanky twenty-year-old.

'We'd need at least seven or eight
good volunteers to do it,' Bat Masterson opined. He was about the same
age as Dixon, and fastidious, always
dressing neatly compared with his
compatriots. 'That might leave this
place short of defenders.'

'I guess we'd know soon enough if
the Indians were moving out from their
village,' Dixon said. 'While they stay in
camp, we're reasonably safe here.'

Terril was excited, feeling certain the
vast supply of buffalo skins at Quanah's
camp could be destroyed, depriving the
Indians of their bargaining power in the
acquisition of guns.

They were sitting in the restaurant

run by Mr and Mrs Olds. The latter, a plain hard-working woman many years younger than her husband, was in pain from an infected tooth, but she refused to give up work, cooking and serving food with her pet crow perched on her shoulder.

'If those Indians hadn't got decent guns,' Terril said, 'the defenders of this place would have a much easier job.'

'When is Armijo likely to return with the guns?' Dixon asked.

'Within the next couple of weeks,' Terril explained. 'He's bound to hide them up some place and then do his bargaining. But he'll never let the Indians have them unless he gets those skins.'

Dixon took a draw on his pipe. 'So what you're suggesting is that we pay a visit to Quanah's camp and set fire to his supply of buffalo skins?'

Terril nodded. 'We'd need to take kerosene to make sure it caught light. And some explosives.'

'Wouldn't be a problem,' Masterson

said, suddenly making up his mind that the risks were worth taking. 'Maybe it would be a damn good investment. Could save a lot of lives all round.'

They talked on, forming a plan, until the stars were fading and the sky in the east showed a lemon flush of light.

At mid morning a meeting of all thirty men present at the trading post was held in Hanrahan's saloon and an agreement reached. Feelings against the Indians were running high and there was no problem in getting volunteers to undertake the venture — Billy Dixon, Bat Masterson, Johnny Tyler, the two Shadler brothers and Billy Ogg and two more men. Terril agreed to lead the party as he knew the exact location of the encampment and the storage arrangements within it.

That afternoon two wagons were loaded with cans of kerosene and explosives. With the remaining men mounted on horses, the party set out and later covered many miles under moonlight. They took a long round-about route that followed a line of bluffs. A further day of cautious travel found them within two miles of Quanah's village. Terril felt sure that so far they had remained unobserved.

At midnight the party was split, the Shadler brothers heading for the eastern end of the encampment with explosives, their intention to cause a diversion which would draw attention away from the storage tents. Meanwhile, those who remained muffled their animals' bits by fastening a loop of rein around the lower jaw. Then they went forward in the kerosene-laden wagons, apart from Tyler, who stayed to guard the horses.

Terril's fear was that the camp dogs would scent intruders on the night air. Sure enough, the animals set up their yapping when the party approached the outer edge of the camp, but at that moment explosions sounded from the far side and an eruption of flame showed against the dark sky. The

Shadler brothers were doing their job.

The result was an immediate exodus of shouting Indians from the tepees, all moving in the direction from which the commotion had come. Most of the menfolk had departed, leaving only a few women and children standing amid the lodges and gazing after them.

Terril waved the wagons forward and they approached the line of tepees which held the valuable buffalo skins. Indians were renowned for being very slack with their guards, leaving dogs to utter warning should there be any night-time intrusions. Now was no exception, and even the canines seemed to have headed off in the direction of the explosions.

The hunters now had to work with great speed before their ruse was rumbled. Staggering under the weight of kerosene cans, they burst into the tepees, scattering the fluid on the stacked hides and generally round about. There were a dozen or more stores of hides and, working in pairs,

160

they had soused the majority by the time Terril struck the first match. Shots were suddenly sounding from the far side of the camp, and he hoped that the Shadlers were not getting more involved than was good for them.

Flames were starting to shoot skywards and the hides were blazing. Some warriors began to return, drawn by the conflagration. Retreating to the wagons, the hunters directed gunfire towards the demon-like figures of the Indians.

The kerosene-induced fire was belching into an inferno and Terril was satisfied that nothing short of a heavenly miracle would prevent the destruction of the hides. He shouted at the others to make haste, to climb into the wagons and get moving. Within ten minutes they were back to where their horses awaited. Thankfully the Shadler brothers were already there.

Soon the entire party was moving briskly back along the path by which they had come. Things had gone surprisingly well. Behind them a huge ruddiness showed against the sky, illuminating the surrounding land. Men's faces glowed in the brightness, all showing satisfaction at the way things had gone. They had been lucky in not sustaining a single casualty. If only that luck could have held.

15

Red Onslaught

In the weeks that followed a lull seemed to descend across the plains. The buffalo hunters continued in their bloody work, although the hides were of poorer quality, having shed their winter thickness. As Terril knew, any pelts now taken by the Indians would be nigh worthless in comparison with the rich supplies that had been destroyed. He took little pride in what had happened, but he knew it had been the most expedient means of cutting Quanah off from his supply of arms, and, as Bat Masterson had said, the action might well have saved many lives.

Terril himself remained watchful, taking up employment in the Myers and Leonard store. At night he dreamed of Armijo, of finding him again, of punishing him. His obsession was not good, but it would not go away. In the evenings he sometimes played monte or dominoes in the saloon, but his mind was seldom on it.

Several wagon trains passed through, stopping overnight at Adobe Walls and dropping off supplies. No doubt his name was now listed on the records of the Texas Rangers, and he knew that if he was recognized and caught a return to prison would be inevitable; so, for the time being, he decided to take his chances at this remote settlement. He did, however, write a letter to Don Antonio, sending it via the wagon train, explaining that Florencia was alive, had married into the Comanche tribe and appeared to be happy.

On three occasions patrols of the Sixth US Cavalry stopped by, and the sight of Federal blue uniforms aroused uneasy memories in Terril. He kept a low profile till the soldiers moved on.

There was also the matter of Diego Armijo. By this time, he must have returned to Quanah's encampment and realized that his no doubt exorbitant deal with the Indians had failed. What his relationship now was with the Comanche chief could only be guessed at. But if Armijo remained in Comancheria, Terril swore he would find him.

On one memorable day he removed the infected tooth of Mrs Olds, while her pet crow, perched on her shoulder and watched in fascination.

And so the spring blossomed into hot summer, and news filtered through that the United States Army was venturing into the Panhandle country with the intention of confronting the Indians and driving them on to the reservation. Terril knew, however, that Quanah had other ideas.

John Terril somehow sensed in his bones that events were due to unfold. Quanah had been inactive for too long. One sultry night in June the residents of Adobe Walls were relaxing, dancing jigs to a fiddle, throwing open their doors and draining the stocks of the saloon.

Terril took a stroll around the outlying corral, saying he would try to shoot a prairie hen or two. Beyond the settlement he sensed a strange ambience over the land. Even the stock showed a restlessness, moving and stumbling as they pulled at the grass. It was as if Fate was holding its breath, waiting for something to happen. From the timber, along Adobe Walls Creek, owlhoots sounded — and Terril was well aware that Indians often communicated with such calls.

He looked for little things — a layer of floating dust in the branches of mesquite, a rabbit or antelope disturbed. He spotted nothing out of place. He chewed uneasily on his moustache.

He chose not to rest indoors that night, but settled down atop a small rise east of the corral, his Henry rifle at hand. He did not sleep much until just before dawn, when he was awakened by the calls of whippoorwills. He gazed out past the grazing stock. A meadow lark rose into the air 300 yards away, circled before flying off. Then something else caught his eye. At the edge of the timber was a dark body of objects, looking like ants, merging in with the shadow. For a moment he was puzzled, then realization slammed into him. He grabbed his rifle and sent a warning shot into the sky.

His shot had an unexpected effect. It aroused the men sleeping in the saloon, but somebody called out that the ridge-pole supporting the roof had snapped. Fearing they were about to be smothered by a downfall of sod, everybody sprang up, gazing at the roof to check its state.

It was then that a hideous war-whooping of warriors shook the morning air and Terril saw how the shadowy figures were fanning out, materializing into feathered warriors, many on horseback. The roar of hoofs and the crack of gunfire added to the alarm. Hundreds of Indians were charging the settlement. The sudden noise panicked the grazing stock.

Terril could see that the wide phalanx of warriors, armed with bows and lances, was heading straight for the buildings, riders whipping their mounts for greater speed. Men and animals were' painted in rich colours of vermilion and ochre. Scalps dangled from bridles, war bonnets fluttered their plumes and the bronzed bodies of the riders glittered with ornaments of silver and brass. The warriors seemed to be charging directly out of the rising sun.

Terril knew it was no time to linger. He ran back towards the nearest building, which was Hanrahan's saloon. Men were scrambling down from checking the roof, still in their under-shirts, now well aware of where the real danger lay. Soon all were inside, Terril with them, the door slammed behind them. They set about barricading the place, using furniture, sacks of flour and whatever they could find to stack against the doors, dragging out boxes of ammunition, loading their heavy Sharps rifles. Terril knew that men in the other buildings were doing likewise.

The Indians burst into the settlement, charging up and down the streets, gesturing with their lances, screaming defiance in the face of the bullets that were directed at them. The noise was ear-splitting. Some warriors rode up to the closed doors, backing their horses into them, thumping against the wood with their tomahawks. They were so close that the hunters' long-range rifles were useless and they were forced to use their pistols.

Terril recognized several of the Indians he had known during his sojourn at their camp, but there was no affection in his heart. He even spotted Quanah himself, directing his force from the centre of the street. He was beating his chest as if challenging his enemies to shoot him. Taking aim through his rifle-port, Terril squeezed his trigger, felt the shock of his rifle's discharge, but the bullet only shattered the buffalo powder-horn the chief was wearing. A second later he was racing down the street through a hail of bullets, clinging by foot and arm to his mount, lifting the body of a fallen warrior as he wheeled away to safety.

Meanwhile, Indians galloped around the buildings, their bullets and arrows thudding against the thick walls. The dust was clouding up. Some dismounted, hurling lances at the rifle slits, waving scalps in the air, screaming obscenities, beating again on the stout wooden doors. A lance came through Terril's rifle-slit, but he saw its approach, dodged to the side; the feathered shaft shot past him, embedding itself in a wooden dresser, quivering like an angry serpent, bringing a mass of bottles crashing down. A few arrows, tipped with fire, also came through, but were rapidly extinguished by the defenders.

Within the saloon, powder smoke hung like a fog, the air was acrid, causing men to cough and rub their eyes. It was difficult to breathe. The heat was suffocating. It was like 'the interior of a Dutch oven full of burning biscuits', as somebody put it. From outside an army bugle sounded, and for a moment hopes of military arrival soared, but then Bat Masterson croaked; 'They got a bugler giving them orders. They're falling back! Quanah's got them drilled like soldiers.'

Gradually the close-in blast of firing subsided; the first onslaught had been repelled by sheer fire-power, each building acting like a miniature fort. But the crack of shots from further afield was audible.

'They're shootin' all our stock and horses,' Billy Dixon said, peering through a rifle-port.

'The bastards,' somebody else proclaimed to general agreement.

'What happened to the Shadlers?' a man called McKinley asked. 'They was sleeping in their wagon down by the creek.'

Terril shook his head. 'I didn't see them,' he said.

McKinley put their dread into words. 'Reckon that was their scalps they was waving at us.'

The faces of the defenders were blackened with gunpowder, their undershirts drenched with sweat. They peered through their rifle-slits. In the street outside, not a single fallen Comanche was apparent, all the dead and wounded had been carried off, though there were smudges of blood in the dust.

Men slumped on the floor, knowing that they had escaped massacre by a hair's breadth — massacre or slow torture to death — so far. Previously, there had not been time for fear, but now some of them were visibly shaken.

In the lull a voice could be heard. Somebody from Myer's and Leonard's store was calling out: 'Johnny Tyler's been hit in the lung! He needs water awful bad.'

Through his rifle-slit, Terril could see an object circling in the sky, looking like a flapping black rag. It was cawing despondently. It was Mrs Olds' pet crow. Such a sight, in view of events, represented an omen of death.

16

Ordeal At Adobe Walls

The thought of young Johnny Tyler, so full of life and fun, dying parched plagued on Terril's mind. He filled four canteens with water from a cask behind the saloon's bar. Somebody said: 'It's a waste of water. If he's shot in the lungs, he's gonna die anyway. And maybe you'll get yourself shot crossing that street.'

Terril did not answer. He corked the canteens, slung them and the Henry across his shoulders and stepped towards the door. Cautiously, Billy Dixon pulled back the barricading so he could get out. Apprehensively, Terril gazed across the deserted street which minutes earlier, had been a seething mass of hate-filled Indians. Now all that was left were the carcasses of two horses, still bedecked with feathers and daubed with war paint. The flies were already drawn to them in clouds. Things had gone really quiet — even the firing from the corral and outlying areas had died out. The way appeared clear. He took a deep breath, then made a dash for it.

He was half-way across when the shot cracked out and by instinct he collapsed into the dust, the canteens clattering about him. Glancing to his left, he saw a brief flash of feathers from some rocks at the edge of the settlement. Immediately, a volley of shots boomed from the saloon behind him, the smoke swirling across the street and all was obscured. He was sodden with either sweat or blood. He was not sure whether he had been hit but there was no time for him to check. He drew himself up, hooking the canteen straps over his shoulders and rushed on. The door of the store, feathered with embedded arrows, opened to receive him and after throwing himself inside, the barricades, sacks of grain, were quickly replaced.

Here was a similar scene to that which he had left; the faces were different but showed the same powder-blackened grimness. Johnny Tyler was lying on the earthen floor, his head resting on a cushion, Mrs Olds bending over him, her lips a tight line of anguish. Johnny looked pale despite the grime on his face, and his eyes were wild with fear. The front of his shirt was bloody. 'Need water,' he wheezed from ruined lungs.

Terril nodded, and dropped to his knees beside him and uncorked a canteen. He poured water into Johnny's reddened mouth, a brief gratitude showing on the boy's face. He swallowed, then a bout of coughing overcame him, and when he calmed and dropped back Terril could see that he was dead.

The remaining water proved popular as parched mouths were moistened.

Suddenly all except Johnny straightened up because the bugle was calling again. It had an unnerving effect.

Mrs Olds murmured: 'God help us!'

Some of the defenders, including Terril, were ex-soldiers and they knew well enough that the bugle was sounding 'the charge'.

Men moved back to the rifle-slits, rifles into their shoulders, eyes straining for the first glimpse of a target. They were not disappointed. The attack was resumed with all its initial fury. Some of the outlying shacks had been set ablaze. Terril tried to glimpse Quanah, but he was not leading his warriors as before. Once again the red tide flooded along the settlement streets; painted, nightmare faces loomed hideously out of the swirling gunsmoke and the Indians were waving scalps in the air, probably those of the Shadlers, trying to lure the defenders out from behind their fortifications, but without success. And within an hour, the onslaught subsided and the attackers drew back. There were no more attacks that day. Contact was established between the buildings of the settlement and provisions and ammunition distributed. Meanwhile, the Indians remained visible on the surrounding hills.

★　★　★

Over the next five days a stand-off existed. The defenders attached telescopes to their Sharps rifles, shooting at any Comanches who ventured into range. They had achieved a sort of victory, but they remained trapped in the settlement, under siege, knowing that if they ventured out, overwhelming numbers would descend upon them. And of course their supplies could not hold out indefinitely — but the fact was that the nature of Indians showed a marked lack of patience.

On the fifth day tragedy struck within the store building. William Olds was climbing down the ladder from the roof when the rifle he was holding accidentally detonated, the charge passing up through his chin into his brain. His wife, so steadfast during the attack, became inconsolable with grief, weeping to an extent that was harrowing to hear. Men stood around, not knowing what to say or do. Presently Terril led her away and sat her down, cradling her head against his chest, feeling her tears flood his shirt.

The only relief that came for her was when her pet crow fluttered back through the window and settled on her shoulder.

Contact between the buildings was now firmly established, and it was decided that somebody should ride to Dodge City and summon aid. Accordingly Henry Lease left during darkness and some days later he returned with a relief force of some forty men. There was now no sign of Indians in the surrounding hills, and subsequently a rumour filtered through that Quanah himself had been wounded in the battle. News also came that the army was stepping up its campaign throughout the Panhandle country to drive the Indians back on to the reservations in Oklahoma.

John Terril now had to decide where his priorities lay; he knew that one false move could land him back in prison. He spent an entire day pondering his options, cleaning and polishing the Henry rifle he had inherited. It had belonged to Mr Olds, but his widow insisted he had it.

He still had work left unfinished. The hateful image of Diego Armijo loomed in his mind.

It seemed that despite events over the last year, he still had no idea of the man's present location. The only real link he had was through the Comanches and Quanah was hardly like to welcome a visit, but the more he dwelt on the thought, the more it seemed the only means of progress. In particular, he longed to be able to speak with Florencia, but of course the last thing he wanted was to put her in danger.

The Indians had certainly stayed clear of Adobe Walls since their abortive attack, but news came through of Comanche depredations elsewhere.

So, Terril concluded, the only key to tracing Armijo appeared to be with Quanah. Through the remainder of the summer, he sought ways of establishing contact, while at the same time hunting the Mexican outlaw. He rode far and wide across the adjacent land, his journeying taking him closer and closer to the Comanche stronghold. Several times he spotted distant Indians, his neck-hair tingling at the sight, but always he kept his distance, knowing that any attempt at communication could cost him his scalp. He forever feared ambush.

The passing months found him no nearer to achieving his aim. Even so, his hatred for Armijo grew, kept pace only by his growing frustration. The deep hurt of losing Josefina still weighed upon him like a heavy stone. Sometimes he would dream that his gaze, centred through the sights of his rifle, swept the land, darting here and there like a brush seeking out that which was unclean. He was obsessed with Armijo. He needed to find him to bring purpose to his life, to provide some justification for all he had suffered.

* * *

Diego Armijo was far closer than Terril imagined. He had cached the weapons he had imported, storing them in the recesses of a secret cave in the Palo Duro Canyon. Despite threats from Quanah, he had refused to trade the weapons for anything less than the agreed 1000 buffalo pelts that the Indians had foolishly allowed to be destroyed. The Comanches had thus attacked Adobe Walls at a disadvantage and paid the penalty, finding no match for the heavy guns of the white hunters. Quanah, himself wounded during the ill-conceived attack, had been furious with Armijo for refusing to release the rifles, had nursed a profound grudge against him since that time. Armijo had long since vacated his lodgings in the Comanche camp, and the bitterness between the two men did not augur well should their paths again cross.

Jealousy flowed strongly in Armijo's veins. He was a hard and dangerous man, but there were times when he wept. He wondered how, if he had married the Baltran girl and benefited from some of her father's money, he would have coped with the different circumstances. He might have become a respected member of society and led a life of luxury. Instead, he had been hounded ever since he had shot the girl and that damn carpetbagger. He considered he had had little alternative but to turn to crime as his means of earning a livelihood, but that did not stop him brooding on the injustices of the past. And he was anxious that those who had wronged him should pay for their stupidity.

Armijo and a dozen of his comancheros, Mexican ruffians, had set up their camp close to the cave housing the stored weapons, but he was aware that he could not stay here for ever. He felt there was money to be made further south, and fancied that a bank robbery in San Antonio might an interesting prospect. But he held the buffalo hunters at Adobe Walls responsible for much of his trouble, firstly with their audacious attack on Quanah to destroy the hides, and then for their resistance against the Comanche attackers. It was time the settlement was snubbed out and he had started to make plans.

17

Stolbred Plays His Hand

The Pinkerton detective with the bushy eyebrows, Stolbred, always made a point of maintaining a low profile. He was dogged in the extreme, sticking to a trail through thick and thin, like a tick that a cow couldn't dislodge. And he had no intention of undertaking his present mission at the behest of Don Antonio Bedran in any other way. His instructions were to find Diego Armijo and arrest him on a charge of murder. He must succeed where others had failed. And his investigations had unearthed a trail and carried him deep into the dangerous Panhandle country. He knew well enough where Armijo was hidden and, by careful observation through his binoculars, had learned of the man's habits — for example how, each morning, he would leave camp and steep his great, hairy body in a nearby stream, leaving his weapons on the bank.

Now, after a week of careful observation, Stolbred decided to play his hand. When Armijo forsook his companions for his early morning dip, Stolbred awaited him. When the Mexican was naked and leaning back in the cooling water, the detective stepped from his concealment, placing himself between his quarry and his weapons, his own gun raised and ready.

'Diego Armijo,' he said, quite gently, 'I am arresting you on a charge of murder!'

Armijo's reaction was not surprising, he sprang to his feet, jay-bird naked, looking as powerful as a bull-buffalo, roaring with indignation. But Stolbred gave his gun an aggressive jerk and the Mexican realized he was looking death in the eye. No words emerged from his open mouth. His great fists were clenching and unclenching, giving the impression that out-gunned or not, he would mangle this impudent upstart just as soon as he came within reach.

But Stolbred was not intimidated. 'You just pull your clothes on and we'll be on our way. I have a horse waiting for you.'

Armijo hesitated, his bearded jaw set stubbornly.

'You better do as I say,' Stolbred persisted quietly, 'otherwise you'll have to ride an awful long way with nothing to protect you from the sun.'

Armijo's eyes glinted dangerously. He cursed, then moved to his clothes at the streamside and pulled them on over his damp body.

Stolbred unhooked a set of handcuffs from his belt, ordered his prisoner to hold his wrists forward as he snapped them on. He worked with long practised one-handedness, his right hand keeping the gun directed at Armijo's head. The cuffs looked puny compared with the Mexican's thick arms, but they reduced the danger of resistance. Kidnap from concealment was something Armijo had himself favoured in the past. Now, for the first time, he was the victim — but he didn't intend matters to stay that way for long.

He loomed over the detective like a giant over a dwarf as they made their way through the trees to where the horses had been left, but Stolbred gave him no chance of trickery.

'You will not get away with this,' Armijo snarled. 'My men will follow.'

'We will see,' the detective murmured.

He forced the Mexican to mount a horse, then linked his ankles by chain beneath the animal's belly. He mounted his own horse, then, leading the second mount by a hackamore, he nudged the way forward. They moved through the hot morning sun, leaving behind the rugged grandeur of the Palo Duro Canyon with its ridges and pinnacles, and travelling across undulating sand-hills. Stolbred did not wish to kill his prisoner, but if he was forced to he would not hesitate. His instructions had emphasized 'dead or alive'.

Armijo had assumed an arrogant, truculent manner, as if knowing full well that this annoying apprehension would only be brief. But the hours slipped by and so did the miles behind them.

It was evening, with the sun sliding towards the far horizon, when a rifle shot sounded, causing Stolbred's animal to rear up. However, the detective quickly regained control, gazed back along the trail and spotted three horsemen following.

'I told you that they would follow.' Armijo grinned.

Stolbred slipped his rifle from its scabbard, worked the lever and fired three shots back towards the men following. As the gunsmoke cleared, there was no sign of his enemies. He gazed for a minute, saw nothing, then urged his prisoner onward with greater haste. Night was hazing in.

They camped that night without fire.

Stolbred did not slacken his vigil for a moment during the dark hours, though Armijo lapsed into a sullen doze. Stolbred usually enjoyed the company of his prisoners, but this man gave him no pleasure.

At dawn they travelled on, Stolbred scanning the back trail for sign of pursuit, but seeing none. Armijo's manner had changed. He was furious at what had happened, furious at his own helplessness.

Just before noon, they topped a rise and saw beneath them the settlement of Adobe Walls.

★   ★   ★

At mid-afternoon Terril returned from one of his circular patrols, disappointed as ever that he had found nothing to indicate Armijo's presence. He rode in, turned his horse into the corral and walked towards the buildings. It was then that he noticed the two unfamiliar horses hitched to the rail outside

Hanrahan's saloon. Apprehensively, he entered. A number of men were present, including Billy Dixon and Bat Masterson, but his gaze was drawn to the two others who were there — both recognizable. Terril's gaze swung from the Pinkerton detective who had arrested him two years ago, and then to the other figure, slumped on the floor, chains about his arms and legs, his wrists cuffed together — his eyes as wild as those of a trapped panther. Shock cut through Terril like a tidal wave. His hand darted for the pistol, holstered at his hip, then paused. There was no immediate danger.

Stolbred replaced his empty glass on the bar. 'How nice to see you, Mr Terril,' he said. 'I heard you got away from that hell-hole of a prison. You needn't worry. I got nothing against you now. I did my job; what the authorities did with you afterwards was up to them. I got bigger fish to fry right now.' He nodded towards the glowering Armijo.

Terril gazed at Armijo and all the hatred rose in him, flooding up into his throat like bile.

'Diego Armijo,' he said, 'you killed my wife.'

Armijo laughed. 'The bitch got what she deserved.' He spat on to the earthen floor.

Pent-up fury exploded in Terril like a bombshell. He sprang towards the Mexican, his fists bunched, but Jess Gosling and Herb Willard grabbed him by the arms, holding him back.

'He'll get what's coming to him,' Stolbred got out. 'Law'll make a better job of it than you.'

Terril shook off those restraining him. Emotion was hammering through him, his eyes smouldering. He fought to control himself, breathing as if he was recovering from a ten-mile sprint. He had combed Texas for this man. He had wanted Armijo in his grasp for so long; he had also wanted to find some remorse, some shame in him for what he'd done. Now he was being denied everything.

But suddenly everything was to change.

The outside door of Hanrahan's saloon had stood open, allowing a breath of air to stir the room, and rays of sunlight to shaft through the hanging dust. Everybody, now, felt the sunlight shadowed. A horse whinnied outside as heads swivelled around. A big man in a sombrero was standing in the doorway, a gun in his hand, briefly cutting off warmth and light like a messenger from the devil. He quickly stepped sideways to press his back against the wall.

'Unfasten him!' he hissed, nodding toward Armijo.

Terril noticed the ugly purple birth-mark high up on the left side of his bearded face. He also noticed that two more men were crowding in his wake, their guns raised threateningly. All three were swarthy Mexicans, unshaven, wild-eyed, crisscrossed with bandoleers. Men on Armijo's payroll!

'Unfasten him — quick!'

Stolbred swore then. Its sharpness cut through the death-ominous atmosphere like a knife. It was the first time he had ever sworn in his life — but he made no move to comply with the order. His owl-like eyes glinted from beneath his great eyebrows.

Terril, standing with one hand rested on the bartop, crouched motionless, conscious that the gun on his hip was only a grab away; he was also aware that any sudden movement would bring a fusillade of lead in his direction.

The scar-faced man pointed his gun at Stolbred, his finger taut on the trigger. The detective knew that death was staring him in the face. With his left hand he produced keys from his pocket, held them up. Suddenly he threw himself to the side, grabbing for his gun. Bullets blasted off, bucketing thunder across the room, shattering the mirror behind the bar. The detective went down, falling across a table, then sliding to the floor, half his gun still in its holster.

Buffalo hunter Abe Jenkins, topped up with liquor, started to drag his long-barrelled pistol from its leather. Like Stolbred, he never made it. The scar-faced man fired into his stomach, doubling him over in agony, blood pumping through his clawing fingers, his scream entwined with the reverberation of the blast. He dropped away, leaving a vision of redness.

The whole world erupted. Terril dived for the floor, seeking flimsy cover behind the legs of a chair. Most of the buffalo hunters were unarmed; their immediate intention to escape the line of fire, stumbling over spittoons, chairs, tables in their panic.

Shots were exploding about Terril's ears, thudding into the thick walls of the room, making the building shudder. Through singing ears, he could hear shouts coming from outside. Horses were whinnying as they pulled against the hitch-rail restraint.

Armijo, still chained, rolled across the floor towards the fallen Stolbred. The scar-faced Mexican rushed forward, grabbed the keys up from the floor. He fumbled to unfasten Armijo, the shackles rattling. The air was filled with the groans of wounded men.

Terril had been playing dead; incredibly, he had been overlooked. Now he went for his gun, thumbed back the hammer, fired into the chest of the third Mexican.

The scar-faced man twisted around from Armijo; he raised his gun and fired at Terril, but the bullet hit the table, splintering off sharp spears of wood.

Armijo was stumbling up, shaking off his shackles. In fury, he stooped and grabbed Stolbred, dragging him to his feet, getting his loose-hanging chain around his throat, his eyes maniacal. The detective was already badly wounded, but now his eyes bulged as the cruel chain crushed his windpipe.

Spinning the cylinder, Terril fired through the acrid air, hit Armijo just above knee, twisting him around, causing him to leave go of Stolbred. Mad with pain, Armijo grabbed Stolbred's gun, fired at Terril, the lead burning across his neck.

The scar-faced Mexican pulled Armijo to his feet, pushing him towards the door. Hanrahan reared up from behind the bar, aiming a shotgun, blasting off, hitting the scar-faced man in the back. Armijo, now alone, hobbled through the doorway, almost falling into the water-trough, leaving a trail of blood behind him. Somehow he reached a hitched horse. He tore the reins free, finding strength despite his bloody leg to haul himself into the saddle. Heels pounding, he was off in a flash, a bullet from Bat Masterson's gun, across the street, only serving to panic his mount into greater speed.

Terril got to his feet, stumbled over the body of a fallen Mexican, but he reached the doorway, seeing the dust clouding as Armijo escaped. Instinctively, he scrambled to the remaining rail-hitched animal, grabbing the reins.

He mustered his strength and climbed into the saddle. Blood was turning his shirt sodden. He knew with certain agony where the wound was — in the same spot where he'd taken a bullet after killing Armijo's brother. He touched it, heard himself cry out. He slammed his heels into his mount's ribs, ramming through the dust in Armijo's wake.

Somehow he had retained possession of his pistol. He fired from the saddle at the departing Armijo but his shots went wide; the hammer finally clicked on an empty chamber.

At the end of the street Armijo's horse stumbled, almost throwing off the outlaw. He was struggling to regain control as Terril drew alongside and threw himself at him. Now both came crashing to the ground, grappling, their hands slippery with blood from their wounds. All the old hatred rose in Terril. They fought like wildcats, clawing biting, knees slamming into groins. Armijo rolled on top of Terril, his weight crushing him, his snarling drowning out all other sound as he grasped Terril's throat.

And that was when Masterson and Dixon and other men came pounding up the street. The butt of Masterson's hard-swung rifle struck the Mexican's skull, beating him into unconsciousness.

Dixon stood over him, the muzzle of his rifle pressed against the outlaw's head, his face tensed for the kill. But Terril gasped out: 'No!' and Dixon hesitated, then drew back the gun.

Terril struggled for breath, panting like a dog. His nose was streaming blood, his face scarred with bite-marks, his body throbbing with pain. 'That'd be too quick,' he managed to explain. 'He . . . he must suffer for what he's done. G-get him chained up again. Get . . . ' His words gave out. He thought he might puke. His strength had gone. He rolled onto his back, gazed up into the sky.

18

Final Destiny

During the days that followed Armijo was given no chance to escape, but held chained under the shadow of a gun barrel, in a storeroom. Meanwhile, Mrs Olds did her best for those who were wounded, including John Terril. The cost had been high. Apart from the three Mexicans who had attempted to rescue their leader, no doubt because he was their paymaster, three buffalo hunters had gone to their graves — Abe Jenkins, Jess Foyle and Jack Wilson. Several more sustained wounds. Adobe Walls would become enshrined as a milestone in the bloodstained history of Texas.

When Terril was sufficiently recovered, he and Bat Masterson loaded the chained Armijo into a wagon and drove him to Fort Dodge where he was handed into military custody. To his dismay, Terril was recognized and found himself locked in the army guard-room, though not in the same cell as Armijo. A week later he was transferred to the jail in San Antonio and he feared he was again destined for the penitentiary. But one morning the keys to his jail rattled, and he looked up to see that he had a visitor, a stern-faced US marshal. Without showing any emotion, he informed Terril that in view of his outstanding service in capturing Diego Armijo, the state governor had signed a declaration granting him a pardon.

Terril slumped on to his cell bunk. He could hardly believe his ears.

* * *

Three months later, Diego Armijo stood trial in the San Antonio courtroom, before the same Judge Emerson as John Terril had faced two years earlier. The Mexican was charged with murder, robbery and rape, and the trial attracted much public interest as Armijo had earned considerable notoriety as a ruthless outlaw. The prosecution revealed far more crimes than even Terril had suspected. Terril was called as witness and felt a chill as he entered the room, but he experienced little emotion as he gave his evidence, stating the facts without embellishment. He had achieved his aim in bringing this evil man to justice, and had no motive left for further retribution. Nothing could bring Josefina back, nor erase his years of terrible ordeal.

Despite his size, Armijo cut a pitiful figure as he stood in the dock. Frequently his hate-filled eyes settled on Terril. He offered little defence; he knew his fate was a foregone conclusion, and it seemed at times that he wished to get matters over as quickly as possible. When the death sentence was passed, he gave an arrogant nod.

Two weeks later he went to the rope before a considerable gathering of prurient onlookers. For some years afterwards his unclaimed, pickled cadaver appeared in sideshows and carnivals, becoming big business as it was gawked at by the curious.

John Terril, deeply affected by all he had suffered, both physically and mentally, frequently soothed his body in the hot-springs, always recalling how he had glimpsed Josefina for the first time as she prepared for her bathe. On other occasions he would find peace at her graveside.

Meanwhile, the Comanche war was far from over. True to Quanah's prediction, the plains ran with blood. Buffalo hunters were slain, isolated ranches attacked, settlements violated, until finally, in a battle in the Palo Duro Canyon, Lieutenant MacKenzie subdued the Indians when his troops killed their horse herd, some 1,500 animals. Only then did Quanah finally make his peace.

Try as Terril might, putting his past behind him was impossible; for a long while he dreamed he was in a room where bullets were flying and men were screaming in agony and he was unable to get out.

Sometimes people asked him about his experiences. They liked nothing more than to sit outside the Ocatillo store, drink coffee, and draw out the story from the reluctant teller. On one occasion, Stolbred, the Pinkerton man, stopped by. He had never truly recovered from his wounds, lead having cut through his shoulder muscle. He had retired from the agency on a pension. They sat for a couple of hours, smoking cigars, sipping whiskey, talking over the past. Afterwards they shook hands, Stolbred departed, and Terril never saw him again.

Florencia lived on the Comanche reservation in south-west Oklahoma, where she was visited frequently by her father. Her husband, White Parker, did not believe in polygamy, and forsook his heathen past to become a Methodist minister. Quanah himself adapted to white ways, though not to the extent that he was prepared to give up any of his nine wives. He became a shrewd administrator and rancher, in due course including among his friends President Theodore Roosevelt.

Meanwhile, John Terril nursed the scars in his memory, allowing them to heal over. He restored his business to its earlier prosperity, attracting customers from far and wide, and he threw open both the doors of his store and of his soul to whatever blessing life might bring.

We do hope that you have enjoyed reading this large print book.

Did you know that all of our titles are available for purchase?

We publish a wide range of high quality large print books including:
**Romances, Mysteries, Classics
General Fiction
Non Fiction and Westerns**

Special interest titles available in large print are:
**The Little Oxford Dictionary
Music Book, Song Book
Hymn Book, Service Book**

Also available from us courtesy of Oxford University Press:
**Young Readers' Dictionary
(large print edition)
Young Readers' Thesaurus
(large print edition)**

For further information or a free brochure, please contact us at:
**Ulverscroft Large Print Books Ltd.,
The Green, Bradgate Road, Anstey,
Leicester, LE7 7FU, England.
Tel:** (00 44) **0116 236 4325
Fax:** (00 44) **0116 234 0205**

THE JAYHAWKERS

Elliot Conway

Luther Kane, one-time captain with Colonel Mosby's raiders, is forced to leave Texas; bounty hunters are tracking down and arresting men who served with the colonel during the Civil War. He joins up with three Missouri brush boys, outlawed by the Union government, and themselves hunted for atrocities committed whilst riding with 'Bloody' Bill Anderson. Now, in a series of bloody shoot-outs, they must take the fight to the red-legs to finally end the war against them . . .

VENGEANCE AT BITTERSWEET

Dale Graham

Always a loner, Largo reckoned it was the reason for his survival as a bounty hunter. But things change when he has to join forces with Colonel Sebastian Kyte in the hunt for a band of desperate killers. Kyte is not interested in financial rewards. So what is the old Confederate soldier's game? And how does a Kiowa medicine man's daughter figure in the final showdown at Bittersweet? Vengeance is sweet, but it comes with a heavy price tag.